PRAISE FOR THE ORIGINAL NOVELLA
THE MAN ON THE CEILING

Winner of the *Bram Stoker Award,*
International Horror Guild Award,
and *World Fantasy Award.*

"All writers of fiction—even we horror writers—avert our eyes at the last moment when confronted with the darkest and deepest core of fear. We are human. We blink. We allow our readers to blink with us. Even scientists agree that it is impossible to stare into a naked singularity and survive. Such a vision is not for mortals.

"In *The Man on the Ceiling,* Steve and Melanie Tem look directly, unblinkingly, into that bottomless well of absolute horror from which all dark fantasy flows. Do not read this story if you are alone. Do not read this story if you are afraid of the truth. Do not read this story if you have ever been afraid of the dark and do not wish to be again.

"As individuals, Melanie and Steve Tem write frequently terrifying and occasionally beautiful tales. Joining their voices in *The Man on the Ceiling,* the Tems have composed a chorus that is at once incredibly frightening, ineffably sweet, and absolutely unforgettable."

—Dan Simmons

"I have only two words for the Tems' *The Man On The Ceiling*: exquisitely compelling. The confessional power, the dangerously arcane secrets exposed, the field of its vision, and the way the story is told . . . well, I have only two words: you must read this. Four words. As good as anything I've read in the last half dozen years, I have only one word for it: simply brilliant. And one word more: Hurrah for the Tem axis!"

— **Harlan Ellison**®

"Melanie and Steve Rasnic Tem have given us a conclusive demonstration that the best horror is open-ended, exploratory, and emotionally truthful. *The Man On The Ceiling* grabs the genre by the scruff of the neck and lifts it right off the ground."

— **Peter Straub**

THE MAN ON THE CEILING

STEVE RASNIC TEM & MELANIE TEM

THE MAN ON THE CEILING

WIZARDS OF THE COAST
DISCOVERIES™

The Man on the Ceiling

Published by Wizards of the Coast, Inc.

Wizards of the Coast Discoveries and its logo are trademarks of Wizards of the Coast, Inc., in the
U.S.A. and other countries. All other trademarks are property of their respective owners.
Printed in the U.S.A.

Book designed by Matt Adelsperger
Cover art by Christopher Gibbs

First Printing: March 2008

9 8 7 6 5 4 3 2 1

ISBN: 978-0-7869-4858-1
620-21726740-001-EN

Library of Congress Cataloging-in-Publication Data
Tem, Melanie.
The man on the ceiling / Melanie Tem & Steve Rasnic Tem.
p. cm.
ISBN 978-0-7869-4858-1
I. Tem, Steve Rasnic, 1950- II. Title.
PS3570.E527M36 2008
813'.54—dc22
2007018090

U.S., CANADA,
ASIA, PACIFIC, & LATIN AMERICA
Wizards of the Coast, Inc.
P.O. Box 707
Renton, WA 98057-0707
+1-800-324-6496

EUROPEAN HEADQUARTERS
Hasbro UK Ltd
Caswell Way
Newport, Gwent NP9 0YH
GREAT BRITAIN
Save this address for your records.

Visit our web site at www.wizards.com

In 2000 American Fantasy Press of
Woodstock, Illinois, operated by Robert and Nancy
Garcia, published "The Man on the Ceiling" as a
novella in chapbook form.
That novella became the seed for this book.
We gratefully acknowledge the Garcias for launching
us on this adventure.

Excerpts from "The Second Coming" by W.B. Yeats by permission of A P Watt Ltd on behalf of
Gráinne Yeats, from *W.B Yeats*, Phoenix Poetry, The Orion Publishing Group, London, 2002.

Santa Claus is Comin' to Town (Vocal)
Words by Haven Gillespie, Music by J. Fred Coots
© 1934 (Renewed 1962) EMI Feist Catalog Inc.
Rights for the Extended Renewal Term in the United States controlled by Haven Gillespie
Music and EMI Feist Catalog Inc. All Rights Controlled outside the United States
Controlled by EMI Feist Catalog Inc. (Publishing) and Alfred Publishing Co., Inc. (Print)
All Rights Reserved. Used by Permission of Alfred Publishing Co., Inc.

For our children, who gave us their blessing

Everything we're about to tell you here is true.

Awake.

Someone in the room.

Asleep. Dreaming.

Someone in the room.

Someone in the room. Someone by the bed. Reaching to touch me but not touching me yet.

I put out my hand and Steve is beside me, solid, breathing steadily. I press myself to him, not wanting to wake him but needing enough to be close to him that I'm selfishly willing to risk it. I can feel his heartbeat through the blanket and sheet, through both our pajamas and both our flesh, through the waking or the dream. He's very warm. If he were dead, if he were the ghostly figure standing by the bed trying to touch me but not touching me, his body heat wouldn't radiate into me like this, wouldn't comfort me. It comforts me intensely.

Someone calls me. I hear only the voice, the tone of voice, and not the name it uses.

Awake. Painful tingling of nerve endings, heart pumping so wildly it hurts. Our golden cat Cinnabar—who often sleeps on my chest and eases some of the fear away by her purring, her small weight, her small radiant body heat, by the sheer miraculous contact with some other living creature who remains fundamentally alien while we touch so surely—moves away now. Moves first onto the mound of Steve's hip, but he doesn't like her on top of him and in his sleep he makes an irritable stirring motion that tips her off. Cinnabar gives an answering irritable trill and jumps off the bed.

Someone calling me. The door, always cracked so I can hear the kids if they cough or call, opens wider now, yellow wash from the hall light across the new forest green carpet of our bedroom, which we've remodeled to be like a forest cave just for the two of us, a sanctuary. A figure in the yellow light, small and shadowy, not calling me now.

Neither asleep nor awake. A middle-of-the-night state of consciousness that isn't hypnagogic either. Meta-wakefulness. Meta-sleep. Aware now of things that are always there, but in daylight are obscured by thoughts and plans, judgments and impressions, words and worries and obligations and sensations, and at night by dreams.

Someone in the room.

Someone by the bed.

Someone coming to get me. I'm too afraid to open my eyes, and too aroused to go back to sleep.

ROAD TRIP

Maybe there are families that have never taken trips of any kind together. But—as son, husband, father, even just as observer—I've never come across a family that didn't have its road stories. The Summer We Went to Yellowstone. The Night Dad Drove the Car off the Road Outside Phoenix. Why Mom Hates Delaware.

For many of us, trips with our families are the only grand adventures we will ever have. Others morph the tedium of the experience into tales gently or bitterly mocking.

Sometimes these memories of family travel are fond. Sometimes they're over-simplified and one-sided cautionary tales explaining why we will never take a driving vacation with our own kids, ever. They become simultaneously inspiration, metaphor, and excuse.

Family life itself is a kind of road trip. Often

the route coincides with the map only occasionally and, even then, deceptively.

Melanie and I have adopted five children over the twenty-five years of our marriage. When they came to us (not all at once), they were four, five, six, seven, and ten.

Sometimes when people ask me how we got them I say we found them along the side of the road—since we'd eaten the last of the fried chicken there was a little room left on the back seat so we said sure, why not, hop on in.

When people ask, "How did you know they weren't going to turn out to be serial killers?" I might rejoin, "How do you know your kids aren't?"

I understand the need to question. Things do get scary out on the road, and practically every responsible person tells you not to pick up strangers.

But I knew they weren't strangers. I knew they were my kids from the moment I first glimpsed them through the windshield, standing beside the road with their flimsy little cardboard suitcases.

"Wasn't it a little dangerous?"

Everything's dangerous. Even in your dreams. Even if you sleep without dreams. From the moment you jump out of bed and take that first breath. Something terrible might happen. Someone's bound to die before the story is over. You might even fall in love.

What I've been telling you is metaphor. They're pretty rare in these parts but some days you can actually bag your limit. I'm told they like to travel in packs for added security.

I love my family beyond reason. The fears I have for my family run beyond reason as well. Traveling beyond the lands of reason you enter the kingdoms of imagination and metaphor. Melanie and I are both professional writers of fiction. One of the many disadvantages of that particular occupational choice is that we've become quite adept at imagining the worst.

As parents, we've also learned that the worst can happen, and somehow the family must go on.

Both as parents and as writers, we've come to respect the imagination, but more than that, to understand just how much a family and its members make their lives there. What might happen next.

What they're going to be when they finally grow up. What their own children will be like. What really happens behind closed eyes, in the middle of a reverie, or late at night when the real world fades into a dream of what happened yesterday.

This memoir—or testament, if you will—is as much a biography of one family's imagination as a chronicle of real life events. It is about both our love and our fear, about what we know and what we cannot know but can imagine. And although what happens in the imagination may be real in a different way than the apparent history of waking events, it is real just the same.

Like memory itself, this testament travels freely through space and time. At one moment our children are youngsters, crawling across our knees. And then, when we're not quite prepared for it, they are adults, with children of their own. We began this story as parents, and are surprised to end it as grandparents, as Grandma and Poppie, as Baba and Papa.

You may wonder what really happened to these people. You may wonder where the day's documentary ends and the dream's journey begins.

I remember driving for a long time that day: ten to twelve hours at least. The kids had been asleep for hours. Melanie had finally dozed off after a long discussion, not exactly an argument, but it had made me tense. I've never done well with conflict, but she never lets me get away with just backing off. Now, I wasn't even sure what exactly we'd been talking about for all that time, but it had much to do, I knew, with our children, and with what I could see outside our car.

Along the side of the road, as far as the eye could see, the children waited. Some of them were babies, owning nothing but the baskets they were in and their own dirty blankets. Sometimes the older kids—and by "older" I mean two or three years of age—would take care of them, holding and singing to them because that came instinctively, feeding them out of other people's garbage cans.

The babies' dreams were elemental. The babies did not dream of parents. They dreamed of warmth and nipples and other good things in their mouths, arms around them keeping them close.

It was the kids old enough to know what families were, or could be, but lacking the cynicism that comes from constant disappointment, who dreamed of parents. Their ideas of what good parents might be were unrealistic, of course, derived as they were from what television shows or movies they had seen. But if there was anything in common in those dreams, it was that the parents were *present*. They did not go away, they did not vanish into some invisible tear in the world.

I looked around the car, at my own children sprawled into haphazard sleep, their bodies twisted as if dropped from a great height. I never had understood how they could find comfort in these positions: Veronica with her hands under her cheekbones and her butt in the air, Chris with his head upside down and hanging off the edge of the seat, Gabriella with one arm raised as if asking questions of some invisible sleep teacher, and Joe with arms fiercely crossed as if trying to break his own rib cage.

And not for the first time I wondered in what nook or cranny Anthony would have found to make his nest, if he had lived long enough to know Gabby and Joe. I wondered if any of my surviving children ever dreamed of him, of how he was or how he might have been. I wondered about what lessons he might have taught them about death, and how they might use that knowledge. There was so much for them to know, or at least to try to understand. Anthony could be a good teacher—certainly he taught me everything I know about loss.

Outside the car windows the children came in droves. Some had barely escaped house fires: you could see places on their necks bubbled like a plastic toy left on the stove. Some had crawled out of floods or earthquakes, their faces smeared and broken. Some stared with eyes that had seen everything but from which nothing looked back when you gazed into them.

There was no more room in the car. I wanted to stick my head out the window and tell them that, and somehow apologize for it, but frankly there were so many I was afraid. Already there were so many, and they were so close, I was afraid I was going to hit one of them so I drove more and more slowly, then sped up for fear of encouraging them to rush the car. That much need, that much evidence of our failure is terrifying. Sometimes I wonder if we will be judged on how we've cared for all our unwanted children and it makes me shudder.

I won't say I wasn't tempted, especially by the ones with something wrong in the face, or something more subtle that still managed to keep them separated out from the rest, as if they might be mythological creatures in disguise, needing someone to champion what was human, and essential in them. I was tempted. But the car was only so big, and I had only so much time, and as it is I don't really know what I'm doing—I'm just playing all this by ear.

"You do what you can." I remember that was one of the things I said to Melanie during our long discussion. "But it isn't enough," is what she said back to me and although I tried to talk her out of that notion I knew of course this is true. How do you live with the fact that the very best you can do isn't enough? I don't know.

We didn't adopt our children in order to save them but that doesn't change the fact that they needed to be saved. We adopted our children because we knew we'd be good parents for them, because already, in a sense, we knew they were ours to parent. Being a parent is not promising you're going to love a child. Being a parent is having sufficient faith, that strong arm of the imagination, to make that child your own, despite everything you know and everything you can't even imagine.

What links our family together is not blood, but that kind of faith. Our children, even though they have come to us out of different failures, different disasters, are brothers and sisters because of that faith, that leap of the imagination that has brought their histories together with ours.

We've done the best we knew how to do. Minute by minute, we're still doing our best. We haven't been able to fix everything.

Despite Chris's innate innocence, he has spent most of his adult life in and out of prison. He does not set out to hurt anyone, but he has hurt a great many people, and I have to admit that I understand him less now than ever.

Veronica has the biggest heart of anyone I have ever known. But the fear she has carried around since she was a little girl, despite our sometimes desperate efforts to heal it, threatens to destroy her time after time.

Gabriella and Joe do well despite their struggles, but they must live with dreams of a birth father who broke his children's arms and fractured their skulls in his fits of rage, and a birth mother who did nothing to stop him.

And Anthony is dead. And we will never know for sure if it was the madness of his first four years that finally caught up with him and ripped him from our lives.

But for just that moment my family was safe, sleeping in their own particular ways. They dreamed of things I was not privy to, but they were safe. All I had to do was pay attention and keep that car on the road.

But you never know what's going to happen on a road trip. You can't always anticipate what you're going to run into.

And the number of desperate children gathering outside the car continued to grow. There's no room, I wanted to tell them. It's all I can do, I might have said, but how could they possibly understand? I looked in my rearview mirror at the other cars, praying they would stop and pick up just a few of those children. But there were so many. You could not begin to imagine them all.

2

ALCHEMY

Imagination transforms one substance into another. It changes what is into what might be, what was into what might have been. Straw becomes gold, gold straw, and neither is more real nor, I submit, more precious than the other. Pebbles turn into luminous pearls and pearls into little gray rocks, both solid and beautiful, both essential. Human beings take shape from clay, angels' wings are spun out of water, fire gives rise to the long tongues of demons, love emerges out of thin air, and the basic elements reconstitute themselves again and again.

Like other powerful tools—language, nuclear energy, genetic engineering—imagination carries risks. If I had imagined my children too vividly before I became their mother, I might have missed who they were and how they would reveal themselves to me. As they grew up, I tried to resist imagining the best or the worst for them (which is to say, my version of the best and worst, not theirs), lest anticipation or worry interfere with meeting them where they were rather than where I hoped or feared they might be.

Anthony did not grow up. One spring evening when he was nine years old, he hanged himself from the post of his top bunk bed with the rope he'd been using earlier to walk the dogs.

I would have imagined that to be unimaginable. Sometimes I still do.

For a while after Anthony died, I sought out the company of other bereaved parents, desperate to immerse myself in their stories and my own. I noticed how the stories often became litanies, told with exactly the same words in exactly the same rhythms:

"When she called to tell me about the accident, we thought it was her son who'd been killed, but it turned out to be mine."

"I knew she was gone before they told me, because her little ears were blue."

"It was the middle of the night when the knock came at the door, and I knew right away that our son was dead."

"When I called him for dinner he didn't answer, and I thought he'd fallen asleep, so I asked Steve to go in and wake him up."

I was struck, too, by how imagination rushes into the miasma of acute grief and does its best to make sense—any kind of sense—out of something not so much nonsensical as a-sensical. Perhaps the need to impose order at almost any cost is primal; perhaps it serves some evolutionary purpose. Any explanation was better than none. In our desperate circle, we created our own myths, which might or might not have been constructed around objective truth, and clung to them even when they caused us harm:

"The school should have known this was going to happen."

"The doctor didn't catch it soon enough."

"If I'd had dinner ready earlier that night, he wouldn't have done it. Five minutes earlier."

"God is punishing me."

"God has broken His word to us."

Was it careless play or suicide? Anthony was not a depressed or angry child; in fact, of all our kids, he was the least volatile. But he had been mad at us that evening because we wouldn't let him go to a friend's house, and he had been horribly abused and abandoned during his infancy and early childhood.

If it was suicide, did he know what he was doing? Is a nine-year-old capable of imagining the finality of death?

Is anyone?

I am. Now.

Knowing the "how" of my son's death became urgent, and my imagination supplied one scenario after another. He'd been playing "doggie" and had slipped off the top bunk. He'd been thinking, with a child's logic, "I'll kill myself, and then they'll let me do what I want." Early trauma had come home to roost.

But the truth is, we'll never know what happened that night or why. And it wasn't until I surrendered to that hard un-knowing that the grief could begin to flow freely. It's still flowing.

So imagination can obfuscate, constrict, trivialize. Imagination can keep us from knowing what's true.

But sometimes imagination is the best or

the only tool available to us for apprehending truth. Before I loved my children, before I met them—before I knew about how Chris would hold my hand when I thought I was going blind, how Veronica would race down a long sidewalk to jump into my arms, how Joe would come and get me to show me a rainbow, how Gabriella would call me "Mommy" well into adulthood, how Anthony would cock his head to the right and sing me a song—before I knew my children at all, they were my children, because I imagined they were.

I did not imagine my children into being. What I imagined—what would not have existed had I not imagined it—was being their mother. I was their mother before we ever knew each other, and they were my children, because of the alchemy of imagination.

It couldn't have been any other way. Some fundamental truths are accessible to us only through imagination. It's magic, and it's as real as it gets.

Usually imagination goes forward. But there's also a form of imagining that, for its own purposes, possesses things from the past.

Everything can be possessed, and has the power to possess. There are places that after-shadow the past in much the way the future can be fore-shadowed—viscerally, with evocation rather than precision, inviting us in to imaginative participation. They come to us through time and space and dimension, demanding—what? Attention, at least. Creative and truthful use.

Increasingly throughout my adult life, I'd had visions of the place of my girlhood. Flashbacks, memory fragments, summonses, breakthroughs from another dimension—I never knew what to call them, and I didn't know whether other people also experienced such things. Vivid, highly sensory, plotless and without characters, they seemed to be about place.

These visions would burst into my consciousness at moments that seemed entirely random and in no way connected to their content. I'd be doing my motherly duty helping one of the kids with algebra homework, and suddenly *white fence blue spruces little marshland along the road, the side yard of the house where I grew up* and then I'd snap back into the present with the sullen child at the dining room table, evidently not having lost any time or space in this reality.

Or, I'd be absorbed in a fascinating lecture about the Anasazi or riparian ecosystems, and *the purple music of a harmonica on a summer's night from the dark porch on the other side of the screen that smells faintly rusty where I press my face against it and close my eyes knowing my father is playing but believing the music has no source* then I'd be back in the classroom with the professor at the same point in the same sentence as when I'd left.

I'd be writing case notes or cooking dinner or watering plants or making love or learning to ski, and *my room when it had gray walls and lavender curtains, the plush of the lavender rug under my bare feet* and then I'd be back and nobody, apparently, would know I'd been gone.

There was an urgency about these visions, but no foreboding. There seemed to be something important in them, but not something dreadful. They didn't frighten me, but they called me, compelled me, though I couldn't figure out why.

The sign says "French Creek Drive," but it's wrong. This road where I grew up does not have a name. "A mile north of town on Route 19, the first dirt road to the left past the gift shop that sells goat's milk fudge, the only house on the left-hand side." The directions come back to me like a jump rope chant.

Despite the sign, I know where I am. I step off the asphalt of Route 19 onto the gravel of the shoulder. A row of ten or so mailboxes used to stand right here, gray metal on splintery wooden poles. Some were shaped like loaves of bread, others like bricks; my family's was like bread. If there was mail, the little metal flag would be up. If it wasn't up, I would check anyway, as much for the ritual of pulling down the stiff-hinged door and reaching into the dusty interior and losing my breath to the wakes of trucks barreling south as for the chance of a letter.

There are no mailboxes now. Adult perspective tells me the poles must have been sunk in concrete; neither my eye nor the scuffing sole of my shoe locates evidence of it, and I wonder if there's any under ground. I wonder how the people on French Creek Drive get their mail. Probably they drive into town to the post office. I'd like to know the smell of the post office, the arrangement of the boxes, likely conversations with the postmaster behind the counter, how many steps lead up to the front door, what time of day sun reflects from the windows and glass door. Maybe I'll stop by the post office when I'm done here.

I wouldn't say I'm frightened. There's nothing to be afraid of here. But the state I'm in does resemble fear—heart pounding, hands shaking, the intense dual sensations of being summoned and of being warned away.

Pledging not to tell myself stories until I've received whatever stories are already here, I set out.

Mrs. Sandbach lived in the first house on the right. I don't remember Mrs. Sandbach, only the name and the house set back from the road in a swampy little bowl. The house is gone now. The ground is still soggy, grass so thick and green-black it might be rotting where it grows. I don't even know how long Mrs. Sandbach lived in this house, when and why she came here, whether it gave her shelter or entrapped her, who ever lived here with her, when she moved or died. I think she died. (Of course she died. She was old then. How old, though? Old in relation to whom? I don't think I ever met Mrs. Sandbach, which is startling.) As far as I am concerned, Mrs. Sandbach always lived here—"always" meaning "all my life," "whenever I took notice."

Apparently our lives intersected for a substantial period of time and space, and did not intersect at all. Unless I was a part of Mrs. Sandbach's life without Mrs. Sandbach being a part of mine. Unless Mrs. Sandbach noticed me. Wondered about me. Watched me going for the mail, waiting for the school bus, running from the mean red dog the neighborhood kids had happily demonized to provide the only danger I was ever aware of growing up.

The possibilities are arresting, along with the realization that I will never know. Standing here at the side of the nameless road, looking at the empty lot, I could make something up. But the story I'm being summoned to and warned away from isn't here, and whatever I made up would not in any sense be true.

The nameless road curves to the left around the

line of tall feathery poplar trees that edged our yard until the year they all died at once—poplars, my father explained grimly, have a short life span—to be replaced by their own ragged stumps. This yard-edge figures strongly in my dreams, daydreams, flashbacks of this place. It's still the only house on the left-hand side, but it's not edged by anything now, no boundary between yard and road. The curve of the road is much shorter than I remember it; I'm around it in much less time. I know not to look yet to the left. It's not time. I'm not ready. I'm not ready.

To the right, off the outside bow of the curve, lies a land shrouded not in Mystery but in lower-case, pleasant, unobtrusive mystery. No intimations of danger or transcendence; my reluctance to go down there has to do with run-of-the-mill worries: I don't live in this neighborhood anymore, and I no longer know where borders of private property are and which ones it's permissible to cross. I would feel self-conscious doing now what once I did freely day after day after day. Out of place.

From the gravel and mud at the outer edge of

the road's curve, I never could see down into the little enclave over the hill, and I can't now. There was a dark brown house in a hollow, and a loose-planked bridge over a rivulet that must have been a tributary of French Creek. A settled place. With no idea who ever lived there, I could make up all sorts of true stories set in that imaginary place, and maybe someday I will. But not now. Now I turn and go on, not looking left.

The Erskines are all dead. Except maybe Bill, Sr.; he's almost certainly dead of old age by now, but I haven't heard about it. Marie, Carole, and Billy have all died of cancer. Maybe Bill did, too.

This knowledge is not new. Carole must have been in her late twenties when she died, and her mother Marie didn't survive her long. I, away from home by then, am not aware of a moment before which I did not know of their deaths and after which I did, although there must have been one.

Billy and I used to listen to cowboy music on his little record player while our mothers chatted on the Erskines' front porch. I used to wonder about Carole, who was older and obese and unpleasant. Marie seemed to cry a lot; I used to wonder about mothers who would weep in that soft, seeping way.

One early-adolescent summer evening, Billy and I sat on my family's picnic table with our feet on the bench, roasting marshmallows in the outdoor fireplace and talking about life. This was the only real connection the two of us ever made, and I'm not sure now how real it was. Real or not, it didn't lead anywhere; we had been childhood playmates solely because of the happenstance of geographic proximity, but we were never friends. I felt no personal loss when he died a few years ago, only an eerie sort of vertigo. Someone sent me his obituary. Small-town newspapers still list cause of death.

Our two families lived just across the road from each other for decades, sharing the same time and place, and I see now that we hardly knew each other, didn't occupy the same place at all. Someone else lives in their house now; there's an SUV in the driveway and a boat in the open garage. Positioning myself to be mostly hidden by the lilac hedge if anybody's looking from the house, my back resolutely to the space where giant blue spruces have, incredibly, been removed from the yard where I grew up, I regard the Erskine house and wonder what it hid then and what it harbors now. Nothing comes to me. Anything I come up with would be out of whole imaginative cloth. After a while I simply move on.

As far as I know, nobody ever even spent the night in the tiny cabin on the creek bank, scarcely larger than a child's playhouse. A few times a year someone—I remember the first or last name Alden and I think maybe he came from Pittsburgh—parked in the truncated driveway, mowed the weeds, and was gone before the sun went down. Although I never saw him arrive or leave, there's no particular mystery about this. It was just a cabin in the country that Alden never used but was obligated to keep up.

But why didn't he use it? Why didn't he sell it? Who was Alden, anyway? How could I have spent my entire childhood across a narrow dirt road from this place and not have known anything about it?

I make a mental note that there might be stories here worth telling. But not today. For me, this little house is not haunted, just empty. I've never been inside it, have no sense of the place it contains and creates, and I'm content to leave it at that.

The Browns lived in a brown house. This word-play made corporeal was a longstanding source of delight to me, the child who lived down the road. My house—long and low like a train, wider than it was tall so that living in a house taller than it was wide became a symbol of emancipation for me—was sometimes pink and sometimes pale green, its color in no way representative of my rather more complicated surname.

Judy Brown was slow. My parents said so whenever Judy's name came up, their voices and faces limned with sympathy and disgust. At the time I didn't quite understand, but now I do remember a certain slowness about Judy, a certain crudeness that seemed to come from simple-mindedness, though it's possible that the memory is really of what my parents said and how their mouths twisted and their eyes cut away when they said it.

There was also something else about Judy, a quality that from the perspective of more than forty years seems to have been wild and joyous, and also hurt, hunted, fearful. As a child I wasn't very good at interpreting facial expressions, but Judy's face would sometimes take on a certain look, her body a certain stance, and I would feel afraid. Not ever afraid of Judy herself, but of what Judy was afraid of.

Judy's brother Buddy was slow, too. He was older. He never rode the school bus. I seldom saw him and never up close, but I knew his skull was pushed in just over his left ear, twisting his whole face; I never heard the story of how that happened to him. When Buddy's name came up, which couldn't have been more than a few times during my entire childhood, something happened in my parents' voices and faces and bodies. Something bad. Something tantalizing. Stay away from him, they warned me, and I did, but I took it as evidence of intolerance and lack of compassion and held it against them for many years, until well after they were dead and things began to fall into a different place.

With long ragged dark hair and a wide mouth, Judy was pretty in a way I recognized even then as coarse, though I wouldn't have the adjective till much later. Judy's stop was next after mine on the school bus route. Flouncing into the seat behind me as if it had been saved for her, she'd lounge against the window with her feet up in what seemed then like wild abandon. One morning she bestowed on me a little blessing. Reaching suddenly over the seat, she touched the mole on my left earlobe and in her loud, rough way pronounced it a beauty mark. And so it was, and so it still is, and when I put in an earring or brush back my hair I smile to think of the kindness of Judy Brown, which has lasted a lifetime.

A long time later, someone who still lives in the area asked me jovially, "Hey, do you remember Wendell Brown?"

"I don't think so."

"He grew up near you somewhere."

"Really? How weird. I'm always sort of shocked to discover everybody in a small town doesn't know everybody. I guess that means I've turned into a real city girl."

"He has like an indentation on the side of his head that sort of contorts his face?"

"You mean Buddy? Buddy Brown?"

"He goes by Wendell now."

"I don't exactly remember him. I remember his sister better, but I don't think Buddy and I had much interaction. He was a lot older than me, sort of a shadowy figure. My parents didn't trust him, I think because he was slow and because of the way he looked. Talk about prejudice."

"Well, he sure remembers you."

"Being so much older, he might remember things I don't."

"To hear him tell it, you two had quite a bit of—interaction."

"What does that mean? I don't remember ever being anywhere near him."

"I probably shouldn't have mentioned it."

"Too late."

"He said you were obsessed."

"With what?"

"With him. With sex. With sex with him."

"You're not serious. I was a little kid."

"Yeah."

"Tell me what he said."

"Actually, what he said was you were a little slut."

One of the things I'm called to witness here is my own visceral reaction. My pulse has quickened. My skin crawls. My throat hurts and my mouth is dry.

It's not fear. I still have no sense of anything terrible. But there's something here. Buddy Brown has something to do with the after-shadowing.

"Where can I find him?"

"I don't know. He moved away."

"Is Judy still in town?"

"Who?"

"His sister."

"I didn't know he had a sister."

I long to ask my parents about this. I've longed to ask my parents about a lot of things. But even if they hadn't been dead for more than a decade, I wouldn't have the nerve.

I have no way of knowing the facts here, and I'm not claiming repressed memory. Buddy Brown is not his real name.

But the images (woods, a little woods, just my size, thin trees and little animals, little singing bird, little snakes just my size) are careening all over the place. I need a shape for them, a receptacle, a (Daddy mowing the lawn right next to the woods, safe smell of cut grass, safe buzz of the lawnmower) story.

So I'll make something up. It may not be factual. It will be honest and true.

JUST HER SIZE

She was playing right at the edge of the woods where Daddy could see her. There was a spider web with a spider in it. She liked how the web felt on her face. She liked knowing that the spider made it.

He wasn't exactly hiding in the woods. He spent a lot of time there, and he watched a lot of stuff, not just her. She was a pretty little thing, even if her eyes were funny-looking and she was a freak like him. Long braids. He bet she didn't have hair anyplace else.

She was looking for a good stick horse. It had to be up to about her shoulders and thick but not too thick and with a fork so you could put a rope on it. This was a little woods, just her size. It just went down to the end of the road. It had little rabbits and moles in it, little birds, little brown snakes, just her size. The trees were all close together. Light came through in fluttery pieces. It smelled wet.

There was a stick. She picked it up and straddled it and galloped right along the edge of the woods. No, it was too long, it didn't go fast enough. A stick horse had to go fast and it had to rear up and whinny. This one didn't. She got off and tossed it into the yard, not a stick horse now, just a stick. Then she remembered Daddy didn't want sticks in the way when he was mowing and she ran out to get it, squealing at the lawnmower pretend-monster, the only kind of monster she knew anything about.

She bet she could find a good stick horse in the woods. She jumped over the line between the yard and the woods, even though there wasn't really anything to jump over, and started along a little windy path just her size. He watched her coming. He'd seen her before, playing in her yard, playing in the woods, and a couple of times she'd said hi to him. She didn't look at him like other people did. She wasn't scared of him, didn't seem to think he was ugly. She couldn't see very well. He watched her coming toward him. She was a pretty little thing, and he knew she liked him.

The path went every which way. You never got

lost in the woods, you just went every which way. She was singing and galloping and making horse noises and tossing her braids. There was that boy. Buddy Brown. She knew who he was. He lived in that brown house. Daddy didn't like him but he was nice.

He said, "Hi."

She said hi back.

He said, "What are you doing?" She said she was looking for a stick horse. He bent down and picked up a branch with a prong at the end of it, stood it on the ground and it came to his waist, her shoulders. "Here's a good one," he said. He was nice.

She came right up to him and grabbed the end of the stick. He used it to pull her toward him, and she didn't try to stop him, she liked him, she wanted what he wanted, little slut, pretty little funny-looking whore.

He put his face down real close to hers and whispered, "I'll give you the stick if you give me a kiss."

She stood on her tiptoes and kissed his cheek, just like that, and he let go of the stick and reached for her, but then her daddy was right there, right behind her, calling her name.

She rode the stick horse away from him to her daddy, and he moved back into the trees and got really quiet, like he knew how to do. They walked right past him, holding hands. She was a pretty little thing.

Is that it? Is that what happened, something like that?

Reversing my steps around the truncated bend in the road, I'm possessed by a spirit of place that I may at last be understanding: danger and protection from danger, all of a piece; several forms of fierce love; things happening before there were words to tell about them. Up at the highway where there are no mailboxes anymore, my ride is waiting. I'm driven to the airport and transported home, to a city neighborhood where all the houses and all the stories are taller than they are wide. Warned by repeated experience that it would be profoundly unsettling, I set it up carefully for both safety and receptivity: I went in the company of a friend who'd long ago escorted me out of that place, someone who lately has been answering the calls of ghosts of his own in order to make a place for himself in a world that once seemed to hold none.

A mile north of town, just past the building that had once been the gift shop with the "Goat's Milk Fudge" sign, we parked just off Route 19 to walk down the road, so I was assured we could escape anytime and stay as long as necessary. My friend stayed close and kept his distance, which may be the very definition of bearing witness.

"Nothing's happening," I kept saying.

Urgent iconic monologue—about Mrs. Sandbach, about the foreshortened bend in the road and the poplars that all died the same year, about dancing to Elvis in the Rogers' kitchen, about Buddy Brown—alternated with urgent, vigilant silence. I marveled at things that had changed and things that had stayed the same and things I didn't remember one way or another. There were a great many of each.

"Nothing's happening," I kept reporting. "Nothing's trying to break through."

The house I grew up in was still the only house on its side of the road. Passing it in both directions, we stopped to stare at it. A car was parked in the reconfigured driveway and the front door off the rebuilt little porch was open, so someone must be home, and I felt like the trespasser I was, standing there looking at someone else's house.

For this was not, of course, the house I grew up in. The place where I grew up is entirely imaginary now.

"I don't exactly know why," I ventured to say, "but I'm at peace with this place now."

I do know why, though. It's because of the story I've told about Buddy Brown. The story has put my childhood home back in its place. The aftershadowing has all but stopped.

The sense of place is a force to be reckoned with. But, as has just been brought home to me again, it's no match for the power of story.

THE MAN ON THE CEILING

47

3
THE MAN ON THE CEILING

Everything we're about to tell you is true.

Don't ask me if I mean that "literally." I know about the literal. The literal has failed miserably to explain the things I've really needed explanations for. The things in your dreams, the things in your head, don't know from literal. And yet that's where most of us live: in our dreams, in our heads. The stories there, those fables and fairytales, are our lives.

Ever since I was a little boy I wanted to find out the names of the mysterious characters who lived in those stories. The heroes, the demons, and the angels. Once I named them, I would be one step closer to understanding them. Once I named them, they would be real.

When Melanie and I got married, we chose this name, TEM. A gypsy word meaning "country," and also the name of an ancient Egyptian deity who created the world and everything in it by naming the world and everything in it, who created its own divine self by naming itself, part by part. Tem became the name for our relationship, that undiscovered country which had always existed inside us both, but had never been real until we met.

Much of our life together has been concerned with this naming. Naming of things, places, and mysterious, shadowy characters. Naming of each other and of what is between us. Making it real.

The most disturbing thing about the figures of horror fiction for me is a particular kind of vagueness in their form. However clearly an author might paint some terrifying figure, if this character truly resonates, if it reflects some essential terror within the human animal, then our minds refuse to fix it into a form. The faces of our real terrors shift and warp the closer they come to us: the werewolf becomes an elderly man on our block becomes the local butcher becomes an uncle we remember coming down for the Christmas holidays when we were five. The face of horror freezes but briefly, and as quickly as we jot down its details, it is something else again.

Melanie used to wake me in the middle of the night to tell me there was a man in our bedroom window, or a man on the ceiling.

I had my doubts, but being a good husband I checked the windows and I checked the ceiling and I attempted to reassure. We had been through this enough times that I had plenty of reason to believe she would not be reassured no matter what I said. Still I made the attempt each time, giving her overly reasonable explanations concerning the way the light had been broken up by wind-blown branches outside, or how the ceiling light fixture might be mistaken for a man's head by a person waking suddenly from a restless sleep or an intense dream. Sometimes my careful explanations irritated her enormously. Still mostly asleep, she would wonder aloud why I couldn't see the man on the ceiling. Was I playing games with her? Trying to placate her when I knew the awful truth?

In fact, despite my attempts at reason, I believed in the man on the ceiling. I always had.

As a child I was a persistent liar. I lied slyly, I lied innocently, and I lied enthusiastically. I lied out of confusion and I lied out of a profound disappointment. One of my more elaborate lies took shape during the 1960 presidential election. While the rest of the country was debating the relative merits of Kennedy and Nixon, I was explaining to my friends how I had been half of a pair of Siamese twins, and how my brother had tragically died during the separation.

This was, perhaps, my most heartfelt lie to date, because in telling this tale I found myself grieving over the loss of my brother, my twin. I had created my first believable character, and my character had hurt me.

Later I came to recognize that about that time (I was ten), the self I had been was dying, and that I was slowly becoming the twin who had died and gone off to some other, better fiction.

Many of my lies since then, the ones I have been paid for, have been about such secret, tragic twins and their other lives. The lives we dream about, and only half-remember after the first shock of day.

So how could I, of all people, doubt the existence of the man on the ceiling?

My first husband did not believe in the man on the ceiling.

At least, he said he didn't. He said he never saw him. Never had night terrors. Never saw the molecules moving in the trunks of trees and felt the distances among the pieces of himself.

I think he did, though, and was too afraid to name what he saw. I think he believed that if he didn't name it, it wouldn't be real. And so, I think, the man on the ceiling got him a long time ago.

Back then, it was usually a snake I'd see, crawling across the ceiling, dropping to loop around my bed. I'd wake up and there would still be a snake—huge, vivid, sinuous, utterly mesmerizing. I'd cry out. I'd call for help. After my first husband had grudgingly come in a few times and hadn't been able to reassure me that there was no snake on the ceiling, he just quit coming.

Steve always comes. Usually, he's already there beside me.

One night a man really did climb in my bedroom window. Really did sit on the edge of my bed, really did mutter incoherently and fumble in the bedclothes, really did look surprised and confused when I sat up and screamed. I guess he thought I was someone else. He left, stumbling, by the same second-story window. I chased him across the room, had the tail of his denim jacket in my hands. But I let him go because I couldn't imagine what I'd do next if I caught him.

By the time I went downstairs and told my first husband, there was no sign of the intruder. By the time the police came, there was no evidence, and I certainly could never have identified him. I couldn't even describe him in any useful way: dark, featureless. Muttering nonsense. As confused as I was. Clearly not meaning me any harm, or any good, either. Not meaning me anything. He thought I was someone else. I wasn't afraid of him. He didn't change my life. He wasn't the man on the ceiling.

I don't think anybody then believed that a man had come in my window in the middle of the night and gone away again. Steve would have believed me.

Yes, I would have believed her. I've come to believe in the reality of all of Melanie's characters. And I believe in the man on the ceiling with all my heart.

For one evening this man on the ceiling climbed slowly down out of the darkness and out of the dream of our marriage and took one of our children away. And changed our lives forever.

But we've made it our job, Melanie and I, to open our eyes and see who's there. To find who's there and to name who's there.

In our life together, we seem to seek it out. Our children, when they become our children, already know the man on the ceiling. Maybe all children do, at some primal level, but ours know him consciously, have already faced him down, and teach us how to do that, too.

We go toward the voice by the door, the shape in the room. Not so much to find the vampires and the werewolves who have been seen so many times before—who are safe to find because no one really believes in them anymore anyway—but to find the hidden figures who lurk in our house and other houses like ours: the boy with the head vigorously shaking nonono, the boy who appears and disappears in the midst of a cluttered bedroom, the little dead girl who controls her family with her wishes and lies, the little boy driven by his dad on a hunting trip down into the darkest heart of the city, and the man who hangs suspended from the ceiling waiting for just the right opportunity to climb down like a message from the eternal. To find the demons. To find the angels.

Sometimes we find these figures right in our own home, infiltrating our life together, standing over the beds of our children.

* * ★ * *

"Mom?"

A child. My child. Calling me, "Mom." A name so precious I never get used to it, emblematic of the joy and terror of this impossible relationship every time one of them says it. Which is often.

"Mom? I had a bad dream."

It's Joe. Who came to us a year and a half ago an unruly, intensely imaginative child so terrified of being abandoned again that he's only very recently been willing to say he loves me. He called me "Mom" right away, but he wouldn't say he loved me.

If you love someone, they leave you. But if you don't love someone, they leave you, too. So your choice isn't between loving and losing but only between loving and not loving.

This is the first time Joe has ever come for me in the middle of the night, the first time he's been willing to test our insistence that that's what parents are here for, although I think he has nightmares a lot.

I slide out of bed and pick him up. He's so small. He holds himself upright, won't snuggle against me, and his wide blue eyes are staring off somewhere, not at me. But his hand is on my shoulder and he lets me put him in my lap in the rocking chair, and he tells me about his dream. About a dog that died and came back to life. Joe loves animals. About Dad and me dying. Himself dying. Anthony dying.

Joe, who never knew Anthony, dreams about Anthony dying. Mourns Anthony. This connection seems wonderful to me, and a little frightening.

Joe's man on the ceiling already has a name, for

Joe's dream is also about how his birth parents hurt him. Left him. He doesn't say it, maybe he's not old enough to name it, but when I suggest he must have felt then that he was going to die, that they were going to kill him, he nods vigorously, thumb in his mouth. And when I point out that he didn't die, that he's still alive and he can play with the cats and dogs and dig in the mud hole and learn to read chapter books and go to the moon someday, his eyes get very big and he nods vigorously and then he snuggles against my shoulder. I hold my breath for this transcendent moment. Joe falls asleep in my lap.

I am wide awake now, holding my sleeping little boy in my lap and rocking, rocking. Shadows move on the ceiling. The man on the ceiling is there. He's always there. And I understand, in a way I don't fully understand and will have lost most of by morning, that he gave me this moment, too.

* ⋆ ★ ⋆ ★

I was never afraid of dying, before. But that changed after the man on the ceiling came down. Now I see his shadow imprinted in my skin, like a brand, and I think about dying. I think about leaving my children without a father.

That doesn't mean I'm unhappy, or that the shadow cast by the man on the ceiling is a shadow of depression. I can't stand people without a sense of humor, nor can I tolerate this sort of morbid fascination with the ways and colorings of death that shows itself even among people who say they enjoy my work. I never believed horror fiction was simply about morbid fascinations. I find that attitude stupid and dull.

The man on the ceiling gives my life an edge. He makes me uneasy; he makes me grieve. And yet he also fills me with awe for what is possible. He shames me with his glimpses into the darkness of human cruelty, and he shocks me when I see bits of my own face in his. He encourages a reverence when I contemplate the inevitability of my own death. And he shakes me with anger, pity, and fear.

The man on the ceiling makes it mean that much more when my daughter's fever breaks, when my son smiles sleepily up at me in the morning and sticks out his tongue.

So I wasn't surprised when one night, late, two

a.m. or so, after I'd stayed up reading, I began to feel a change in the air of the house, as if something were being added, or something taken away.

Cinnabar uncurled and lifted her head, her snout wrinkling as if to test the air. Then her head turned slowly atop her body, and her yellow eyes became silver as she made a long, motionless stare into the darkness beyond our bedroom door. Poised. Transfixed.

I glanced down at Melanie sleeping beside me. I could see Cinnabar's claws piercing the sheet and yet Melanie did not wake up. I leaned over her then to see if I could convince myself she was breathing. Melanie breathes so shallowly during sleep that half the time I can't tell she's breathing at all. So it isn't unusual to find me poised over her like this during the middle of the night, like some anxious and aging gargoyle, waiting to see the rise and fall of the covers to let me know she is still alive. I don't know if this is normal behavior or not—I've never really discussed it with anyone before. But no matter how often I watch my wife like this, and wait, no matter how often I see that yes, she is breathing, I still find myself considering what I would do, how I would feel, if that miraculous breathing did stop. Every time I worry myself with an imagined routine of failed attempts to revive her, to put the breathing back in, of frantic late night calls to anyone who might listen, begging them to tell me what I should do to put the breathing back in. It would be my fault, of course, because I had been watching. I should have watched her more carefully. I should have known exactly what to do.

During these ruminations I become intensely aware of how ephemeral we are. Sometimes I think we're all little more than a ghost of a memory, our flesh a poor joke.

I also become painfully aware of how, even for me when I'm acting the part of the writer, the right words to express just how much I love Melanie are so hard to come by.

At that point, the man on the ceiling stuck his head through our bedroom door and looked right at me. He turned, looking at Melanie's near-motionless form—and I saw how thin he was, like a silhouette cut from black construction paper. Then he pulled his head back into the darkness and disappeared.

I eased out of bed, trying not to awaken Melanie. Cinnabar raised her back and took a swipe at me. I moved toward the doorway, taking one last look back at the bed. Cinnabar stared at me as if she couldn't believe I was actually doing this, as though I were crazy.

For I intended to follow the man on the ceiling and find out where he was going. I couldn't take him lightly. I already knew some of what he was capable of. So I followed him that night, as I have followed him every night since, in and out of shadow, through dreams and memories of dreams, down the back steps and up into the attic, past the fitful or peaceful sleep of my children, through daily encounters with death, forgiveness, and love.

Usually he is this shadow I've described, a silhouette clipped out of the dark, a shadow of a shadow. But these are merely the aspects I'm normally willing to face. Sometimes as he glides from darkness into light and into darkness again, as he steps and drifts through the night rooms and corridors of our house, I glimpse his figure from other angles: a mouth suddenly fleshed out and full of teeth, eyes like the devil's eyes like my own father's eyes, a hairy fist with coarse fingers, a jawbone with my own beard attached.

And sometimes his changes are more elaborate: he sprouts needle teeth, razor fingers, or a mouth like a swirling metal funnel.

The man on the ceiling casts shadows of flesh, and sometimes the shadows take on a life of their own.

* * ★ * *

Many years later, the snake returned. I was very awake. Steve wasn't home.

I'd been offered painkillers and tranquilizers to produce the undead state which often passes for grieving but is not. I refused them. I wanted to be awake. The coils of the snake dropped from the ceiling and rose from the floor—oozing, slithering, until I was entirely encased. The skin molted and molted again into my own skin. The flesh was supple around my own flesh. The color of the world from inside the coils of the snake was a growing, soothing green.

"Safe," hissed the snake all around me. "You are safe."

Everything we're telling you here is true.

* * ✹ * *

Each night as Melanie sleeps, I follow the man on the ceiling into the various rooms of my children and watch him as he stands over them, touches them, kisses their cheeks with his black ribbon tongue. I imagine what he must be doing to them, what transformations he might be orchestrating in their dreams.

I imagine him creeping up to my youngest daughter's bed, reaching out his narrow black fingers and like a razor they enter her skull so he can change things there, move things around, plant ideas that might sprout—deadly or healing—in years to come. She is seven years old, and an artist. Already her pictures are thoughtful and detailed and she's not afraid of taking risks: cats shaped like hearts, people with feathers for hair, roses made entirely of concentric arcs. Does the man on the ceiling have anything to do with this?

I imagine him crawling into bed with my youngest son, whispering things into my son's ear, and suddenly my son's sweet character has changed forever.

I imagine him climbing the attic stairs and passing through the door to my teenage daughter's bedroom without making a sound, slipping over her sleeping form so gradually it's as if a car's headlights had passed and the shadows in the room had shifted and now the man from the ceiling is kissing my daughter and infecting her with a yearning she'll never be rid of.

I imagine him flying out of the house altogether, leaving behind a shadow of his shadow who is no less dangerous than he is, flying away from our house to find our troubled oldest son, filling his head with thoughts he won't be able to control, filling his brain with hallucinations he won't have to induce, imprisoning him forever where he is now imprisoned.

Every night since that first night the man on the ceiling climbed down, I have followed him all evening like this: in my dreams, or sitting up in bed, or resting in a chair, or poised in front of a computer screen typing obsessively, waiting for him to reveal himself through my words.

Our teenage daughter has night terrors. I suspect she always has. When she came to us a tiny and terrified seven-year-old, I think the terrors were everywhere, day and night. When I was a girl I had the usual child's nightmares, but nothing like that.

Now she's sixteen, and she's still afraid of many things. Her strength, her wisdom beyond her years, is in going toward what frightens her. I watch her do that, and I am amazed. She worries, for instance, about serial killers, and so she's read and re-read everything she could find about Ted Bundy, Jeffrey Dahmer, John Wayne Gacy. She's afraid of death, partly because it's seductive, and so she wants to be a mortician or a forensic photographer—get inside death, see what makes a dead body dead, record the evidence. Go as close to the fear as you can. Go as close to the monster. Know it. Claim it. Name it. Take it in.

She's afraid of love, and so she falls in love often and deeply.

Her night terrors now most often take the form

of a faceless lady in white who stands by her bed with a knife and intends to kill her, tries to steal her breath the way they used to say cats would do if you let them near the crib. The lady doesn't disappear even when our daughter wakes herself up, sits up in bed and turns on the light.

Our daughter wanted something alive to sleep with. The cats betrayed her, wouldn't be confined to her room. So we got her a dog. Ezra was abandoned, too, or lost and never found, and he's far more worried than she is, which I don't think she thought possible. He sleeps with her. He sleeps under her covers. He would sleep on her pillow, covering her face, if she'd let him, and she would let him if she could breathe. She says the lady hasn't come once since Ezra has been here.

I don't know if Ezra will keep the night terrors away forever. But, if she trusts him, he'll let her know whether the lady is real. That's no small gift.

Our daughter is afraid of many things, and saddened by many things. She accepts pain better than most people, takes in pain. I think that now her challenge, her adventure, is to learn to accept happiness. That's scary.

THE MAN ON THE CEILING

So maybe the lady at the end of her bed doesn't intend to kill her after all. Maybe she intends to teach her how to take in happiness.

Which is, I guess, a kind of death.

* * ★ * *

I know that the lady beside my daughter's bed is real, but this is not something I have yet chosen to share with my daughter. I saw this lady in my own night terrors when I was a boy, just as I saw the devil in my bedroom one night in the form of a giant goat, six feet tall at the shoulder. I sat up in my bed and watched as the goat's body disappeared slowly, one layer of hair and skin at a time, leaving giant, bloodshot, humanoid eyes, the eyes of the devil, suspended in mid-air where they remained for several minutes while I gasped for a scream that would not come.

I had night terrors for years until I began experimenting with dream control and learned to extend myself directly into a dream where I could rearrange its pieces and have things happen the way I wanted them to happen. Sometimes when I write now it's as if I'm in the midst of this extended night terror and I'm frantically using powers of the imagination I'm not even sure belong to me to arrange the pieces and make everything turn out the way it should, or at least the way I think it was meant to be.

If the man on the ceiling were just another night terror, I should have the necessary tools to stop him in his tracks, or at least to divert him. But I've followed the man on the ceiling night after night. I've seen what he does to my wife and children. And he's already carried one of our children away.

Remember what I said in the beginning. Everything we're telling you here is true.

I follow the man on the ceiling around the attic of our house, my flashlight burning off pieces of his body, which grow back as soon as he moves beyond the beam. I chase him down three flights of stairs into our basement where he hides in the laundry. My hands turn into frantic paddles that scatter the clothes and I'm already thinking about how I'm going to explain the mess to Melanie in the morning when he slips like a pool of oil under my feet and out to other corners of the basement where my children keep their toys. I imagine the edge of his cheek in an oversized doll, his amazingly sharp fingers under the hoods of my son's Matchbox cars.

But the man on the ceiling is a story and I know something about stories. One day I will figure out just what this man on the ceiling is "about." He's a character in the dream of our lives and he can be changed or killed.

* * ★ * *

It always makes me cranky to be asked what a story is "about," or who my characters "are." If I could tell you, I wouldn't have to write them.

I don't much like it, either, when Steve is asked how he could possibly write from a female point of view. (Notably, I've never been asked how I can write from a male point of view.)

Often I write about people I don't understand, ways of being in the world that baffle me. I want to know how people make sense of things, what they say to themselves, how they live. How they name themselves to themselves.

Because life is hard. Even when it's wonderful, even when it's beautiful—which it is a lot of the time—it's hard. Sometimes I don't know how any of us makes it through the day. Or the night.

The world has in it: Children hurt or killed by their parents, who would say they do it out of love. Children whose beloved fathers, uncles, brothers, cousins, mothers love them, too, fall in love with them, say anything we do to each other's bodies is okay because we love each other, but don't tell anybody because then I'll go to jail and then I won't love you anymore.

Perverted love.

The world also has in it: Children whose only chance to grow up is in prison, because they're afraid to trust love on the outside. Children who die, no matter how much you love them.

Impotent love.

And the world also has in it: Werewolves, whose unclaimed rage transforms them into something not human but also not inhuman (modern psychiatry sometimes finds the bestial "alter" in the multiple personality). Vampires, whose unbridled need to experience leads them to suck other people dry and are still not satisfied. Zombies, the chronically insulated, people who will not feel anything because they will not feel pain. Ghosts.

I write in order to understand these things. I

write dark fantasy because it helps me see how to live in a world with monsters.

But one day last week, transferring at a crowded and cold downtown bus stop, late as usual, I was searching irritably in my purse for my bus pass, which was not there, and then for no reason and certainly without conscious intent my gaze abruptly lifted and followed the upswept lines of the pearly glass building across the street, up, up, into the Colorado-blue sky, and it was beautiful.

It was transcendently beautiful. An epiphany. A momentary breakthrough into the dimension of the divine.

That's why I write, too. To stay available for breakthroughs into the dimension of the divine. Which happen in this world all the time.

I think I always write about love.

* ⋆ ✶ ⋆ *

I married Melanie because she uses words like "divine" and "transcendent" in everyday conversation. I love that about her. It scares me, and it embarrasses me sometimes, but still I love that about her. I was a secretive and frightened male, perhaps like most males, when I met her. And now sometimes even I will use a word like "transcendent." I'm still working on "divine."

And sometimes I write about love. Certainly I love all my characters, miserable lot though they may be. (Another writer once asked me why I wrote about "nebbishes." I told him I wanted to write about "the common man.") Sometimes I even love the man on the ceiling, as much as I hate him, because of all the things he enables me to see. Each evening, carrying my flashlight, I follow him through all the dark rooms of my life. He doesn't need a light because he has learned these rooms so well and because he carries his own light. If you'll look at him carefully you'll notice that his grin glows in the darkness. I follow him because I need to understand him. I follow him because he always has something new to show me.

One night I followed him into a far corner of our attic. Apparently that was where he slept when he wasn't clinging to our ceiling or prowling our children's rooms. He had made himself a nest out of old photos chewed up and their emulsions spat out into a paste to hold together bits of outgrown clothing and the gutted stuffing of our children's discarded dolls and teddy bears. He lay curled up, his great dark sides heaving.

I flashed the light on him. And then I saw his wings

They were patchwork affairs, the separate sections molded out of burnt newspaper, ancient lingerie, metal road signs, and fish nets, stitched together with shoelaces and Bubble Yum, glued and veined with tears, soot, and ash. The man on the ceiling turned his obsidian head and blew me a kiss of smoke.

I stood perfectly still with the light in my hand growing dimmer as he drained away its brightness. So the man on the ceiling was in fact an angel, a messenger between our worldly selves and—yes, I'll say it—the divine. And it bothered me that I hadn't recognized his angelic nature before. I should have known, because aren't ghosts nothing more than angels with wings of memory, and vampires angels with wings of blood?

Everything we're trying to tell you here is true.

And there are all kinds of truths to tell. There's the true story about how the man, the angel, on the ceiling killed my mother, and what I did with her body. There's the story about how my teenage daughter fell in love with the man on the ceiling and ran away with him and we didn't see her for weeks. There's the story about how I tried to become the man on the ceiling in order to understand him and ended up terrorizing my own children.

There are so many true stories to tell. So many possibilities.

There are so many stories to tell. I could tell this story about myself, or someone masquerading as myself:

Penguins

Melanie smiled at the toddler standing up backward in the seat in front of her. He wasn't holding
onto anything, and his mouth rested dangerously on
the metal bar across the back of the seat. His mother
couldn't have been much more than seventeen, from
what Melanie could see of her pug-nosed, rouged
and sparkly-eye-shadowed, elaborately poufed profile. Melanie was hoping it was his big sister until
she heard him call her, "Mama."

"Mama," he kept saying. "Mama. Mama." The
girl ignored him. His prattle became increasingly
louder and more shrill until everyone on the bus
was looking at him, except his mother, who had
her head turned as far away from him as she could.
She was cracking her gum.

The sunset was lovely, peach and purple and
gray, made more lovely by the streaks of dirt on
the bus windows and by the contrasting bright

white dots of headlights and bright red dots of tail lights moving everywhere under it. When they passed slowly over the Valley Highway, Melanie saw that the lights were exquisite, and hardly moving at all.

"Mama! Mama! Mama!" The child swiveled clumsily toward his mother and reached out both hands for her just as the driver hit the brakes. The little boy toppled sideways and hit his mouth on the metal bar. A small spot of blood appeared on his lower lip. There was a moment of stunned silence from the child; his mother—still staring off away from him, earphones over her ears, still popping her gum rhythmically—obviously hadn't noticed what had happened.

Then he shrieked. At last disturbed, she whirled on him furiously, an epithet halfway out of her child-vamp mouth, but when she saw the blood on her son's face she collapsed into near-hysteria. Although she did hold him and wipe at his face with her long-nailed fingertips, it was clear she didn't know what to do.

Melanie considered handing her a tissue, lecturing her about child safety, even—ridiculously—calling social services. But here was her stop. Fuming, she followed the lady with the shoulder-length white hair down the steps and out into the evening, which was tinted peach and purple and gray from the sunset of however dubious origin and, no less prettily, red and white from the Safeway sign.

The white-haired woman was always on this bus. Always wore the same ankle-length red coat when it was cold enough to wear any coat at all. Grim-faced and always frowning, but with that crystalline hair falling softly over her shoulders.

They always got off at the same stop, waited at the intersection for the light to change, walked together a block and a half until the lady turned into the Spanish-style stucco apartment building that had once been a church—it still had "Jesus Is the Light of the World" inscribed in an arc over one doorway and a pretty enclosed courtyard overlooked by tall windows shaped as if to hold stained glass. At that point, Melanie's house was still two blocks away, and she always just kept walking. She and the white-haired lady had never exchanged a word. Maybe someday she'd think how to start a conversation. Not tonight.

Tonight, like most nights, she just wanted to be home. Safe and patently loved in the hubbub of her family. Often, disbelieving, she would count to herself the number of discrete living creatures whose lives she shared, and she loved the changing totals: tonight it was Steve, and five kids, four cats, three dogs, even twenty-three plants. Exhausted from work, she could almost always count on being revitalized when she went home.

The man on the ceiling laughs at me as he remains always just out of the reach of my understanding, floating above me on his layered wings, telling me about how, someday, Melanie and my children and everyone I love is going to die and how, after I die, no one is going to remember me no matter how much I write, how much I shamelessly reveal, brushing his sharp fingers against the wallpaper and leaving deep gouges in the walls. He rakes back the curtains and shows me the sky: peach and purple and gray like the colors of his eyes when he opens them, like the colors of his mouth, the colors of his tongue when he laughs even more loudly and heads for the open door of one of my children's rooms.

The man on the ceiling opens his mouth and begins eating the wall by the staircase. First he has to taste it. He rests the dark holes that have been drilled into his face for nostrils against the brittle flocked wallpaper and sniffs out decades worth of noise, conversation, and prayers. Then he slips his teeth over the edges and pulls it away from the wall, shoveling the crackling paper into his dark maw with fingers curved into claws. Tiny trains of silverfish drift down the exposed wall before the man on the ceiling devours them as well, then his abrasive tongue scoops out the crumbling plaster from the wooden lath and minutes later he has started on the framing itself.

Powerless to stop him, I watch as he sups on the dream of my life. Suddenly I am a sixteen-year-old boy again and this life I have written for myself is all ahead of me, and impossibly out of reach.

The man on the ceiling turns and screams at me until I feel my flesh beginning to shred. The man on the ceiling puts his razor-sharp fingers into my joints and twists and I clench my fists and bite the insides of my lips trying not to scream. The man on the ceiling grins and grins and grins. He sticks both hands into my belly and pulls out my organs and offers to tell me how long I have to live.

I tell him I don't want to know, and then he offers to tell me how long Melanie is going to live, how long each of my children is going to live.

The man on the ceiling crawls into my belly through the hole he has made and curls up inside himself to become a cancer resting against my spinal column. I can no longer walk and I fall to the ground.

The man on the ceiling rises into my throat and I can no longer speak. The man on the ceiling floats into my skull and I can no longer dream.

The man on the ceiling crawls out of my head, his sharp black heels piercing my tongue as he steps out of my mouth.

The man on the ceiling starts devouring our furniture a piece at a time, beating his great conglomerate wings in orgasmic frenzy, releasing tiny gifts of decay into the air.

How might I explain why supposedly good people could imagine such things? How might I explain how I could feel such passion for my wife and children, or for the simplest acts of living, when such creatures travel in packs through my dreams?

It is because the man on the ceiling is a true story that I find life infinitely interesting. It is because of such dark, transcendent angels in each of our houses that we are able to love. Because we must. Because it is all there is.

Penguins

Daffodils were blooming around the porch of the little yellow house set down away from the sidewalk. Melanie stopped, amazed. They had not been there yesterday. Their scent lasted all the way to the corner.

One year Steve had given her a five-foot-long, three-foot-high Valentine showing a huge flock of penguins, all of them alike, and out of the crowd two of them with pink hearts above their heads, and the caption: "I'm so glad we found each other." It was, of course, a miracle.

She crossed the street and entered her own block. The sunset was paling now, and the light was silvery down the street. A trick of the light made it look as though the hill on which her house sat was flattened. Melanie smiled and wondered what Matilda McCollum, who'd had the house built in 1898 and had the hill constructed so it would be grander than her sister's otherwise identical house across the way, would say to that. A huge, solid, sprawling, red-brick Victorian rooted in Engelmann ivy so expansive as to be just this side of overgrown, the house was majestic on its hill. Grand. Unshakable. Matilda had been right.

Melanie was looking left at the catalpa tree between the sidewalk and the street, worrying as she did every spring that this time it really would never leaf out and she would discover it was dead, had died over the winter and she hadn't known, had in fact always been secretly dead, when she turned right to go up the steps to her house. Stumbled. Almost fell. There were no steps. There was no hill. She looked up. There was no house.

And she knew there never had been.

There never had been a family. She had never had children.

She had somehow made up sweet troubled Christopher, Veronica of the magnificent chestnut hair and heart bursting painfully with love, Anthony whose laughter had been like seashells, Joe for

whom the world was an endless adventure, Gabriella who knew how to go inside herself and knew
to tell you what she was doing there: "I be calm."

She'd made up the golden cat Cinnabar, who
would come to purr on her chest and ease the pain
away. She'd made up the hoya plant that sent out
improbable white flowers off a leafless woody stem
too far into the dining room. She'd made up the
rainbows on the kitchen walls from the prisms she
hung in the south window.

She'd made up Steve.

There had never been love.

There had never been a miracle.

Angels. Our lives are filled with angels.

The man on the ceiling smiles in the midst of the emptiness, his wings beating heavily against the clouds, his teeth the color of the cold I am feeling now. Melanie used to worry so much when I went out late at night for milk, or ice cream for the both of us, that I'd need to call her from a phone booth if I thought I'd be longer than the forty-five minutes it took for her anxiety and her fantasies about all that can happen to people to kick in. Sometimes she fantasized about the police showing up at the door to let her know about the terrible accident I'd had, or sometimes I just didn't come back—I got the milk or the ice cream and I just kept on going. I can't say that I was always helpful. Sometimes I'd tell her I had to come home because the ice cream would melt if I didn't get it into the freezer right away. I'm not sure that was very reassuring.

What I tried not to think about was what if I never could find my way home, what if things weren't as I'd left them. What if everything had changed? One night I got lost along the southern edge of the city after a late night movie and wandered for an hour or so convinced that my worst fantasies had come true.

The man on the ceiling smiles and begins devouring my dream of the sky.

* * ★ * ★

A wise man asks me, when I've told him this story of my vanishing home again, "And then what?"

I glare at him. He's supposed to understand me. "What do you mean?"

"And then what happens? After you discover that your house and your husband and your family have disappeared?"

"Not disappeared," I point out irritably. "Have never existed."

"Yes. Have never existed. And then what happens?"

I've never thought of that. The never-having-existed seems final enough, awful enough. I can't think of anything to say, so I don't say anything, hoping he will. But he's wise, and he knows how to use silence. He just sits there, being calm, until finally I say, "I don't know."

"Maybe it would be interesting to find out," he suggests.

So we try. He eases me into a light trance; I'm eager and highly suggestible, and I trust this man, so my consciousness alters easily. He guides me through the fantasy again and again, using my own words and some of his own. But every time I stop at the point where I come home and there isn't any home. The point where I look up and my life, my love, isn't there. Has never existed.

I don't know what happens next. I can't imagine what happens next. Do I die? Does the man on the ceiling take me into his house? Does he fly away with me into an endless sky? Does he help me create another life, another miracle?

That's why I write. To find out what happens next.

* ✱ * ✱

So what happens next? This might happen:

After the man on the ceiling devours my life I

imagine it back again: I fill in the walls, the doorways, the empty rooms with colors and furnishings different from, but similar to, the ones I imagine to have been there before. Our lives are full of angels of all kinds. So I call on some of those other angels to get my life back.

I write myself a life, and it is very different from the one I had before, and yet very much the same. I make mistakes different from the ones I made with my children before. I love Melanie the same way I did before. Different wonderful things happen. The same sad, wonderful events recur.

The man on the ceiling just smiles at me and makes of these new imaginings his dessert. So what happens next? In a different kind of story I might take out a machete and chop him into little bits of shadow. Or I might blast him into daylight with a machine gun. I might douse him with lighter fluid and set him on fire.

But I don't write those kinds of stories.

And besides, the man on the ceiling is a necessary angel.

There are so many truths to tell. There are so many different lives I could dream for myself.

What happens next?

There are so many stories to tell. I could tell this story:

The man on the ceiling was waiting for Melanie behind the fence (an ugly, bare, chain link and chicken wire fence, not the black wrought iron fence plaited with rosebushes that she'd made up), where her home had never existed. He beckoned to her. He called her by name, his own special name for her, a name she never got used to no matter how often he said it, which was often. He reached for her, trying to touch her but not quite touching.

She could have turned and run away from him. He wouldn't have chased her down. His arms wouldn't have telescoped long and impossibly jointed to capture her at the end of the block. His teeth wouldn't have pushed themselves out of his mouth in gigantic segmented fangs to cut her off at the knees, to bite her head off. He wouldn't have sucked her blood.

But he'd have kept calling her, using his special name for her. And he'd have scaled her windows, dropped from her roof, crawled across her ceiling again that night, and every night for the rest of her life.

So Melanie went toward him. Held out her arms.

* ✦ ★ ✦ *

There are so many different dreams. That one was Steve's. This one is mine:

I sit down at the kitchen table. The man on the ceiling lies on my plate, collapsed and folded up neatly in the center. I slice him into hundreds of oily little pieces which I put into my mouth one morsel at a time. I bite through his patchwork wings. I gnaw on his inky heart. I chew his long, narrow fingers well. I make of him my daily meal of darkness.

* ✦ ★ ✦ *

There are so many stories to tell.

And all of the stories are true.

We wait for whatever happens next.

We stay available.

We name it to make it real.

It was hard for us to write this piece.

For one thing, we write differently. Melanie's stories tend more toward magical realism, Steve's more toward surrealism. Realism, in both cases, but we argued over form: "This isn't a story! It doesn't have a plot!"

"What do you want from a plot? Important things happen, and it does move from A to B."

In our fiction, Melanie's monsters usually are ultimately either vanquished or accepted, while at the end of Steve's stories you often find out that the darkness in one form or another lives on and on. There's no escaping it, and the question is whether you should try to escape it in the first place.

Since words can only approximate both the monsters and the vanquishment, we wrote each other worried notes in the margins of this story.

"I don't know if we can really use the word 'divine.'"

"If someone looked inside your dreams, would they really see only darkness?"

It was hard for us to write this piece.

"This upsets me," Melanie would say.

Steve would nod. "Maybe we can't do this."

"Oh, we have to." Melanie would insist. "We've gone too far to stop now. I want to see what happens."

This piece is about writing and horror and fear and about love. We're utterly separate from each other, of course, yet there's a country we share, a rich and wonderful place, a divine place, and we create it by naming all of its parts, all of the angels and all of the demons who live there with us.

What happens next?

There are so many stories to tell.

We could tell another story:

4
SENSE OF PLACE

I've been accused of worrying too much, of seeing layers of darkness other people could not see, of perceiving horrors the way dogs hear sounds imperceptible to humans. I've been too quick at times, I'm told, to lose faith in the safety of a place, a time, or another human being.

But then I hear a story like Melanie's story of Buddy, and it rings so true, it jibes so closely with other stories I've heard or sifted out of all the messy details that fall between the lines.

There are bad people out there—sometimes there are bad people living next door. You must understand this. And there's not always something you can do about it. It's tempting to fantasize about fixing the bad things that have already happened, might have happened, such as going back in time and pulling the little girl Melanie out of harm's way, and telling her father, because

THE MAN ON THE CEILING

101

this is just the sort of information fathers need to know. However much they might try, fathers do not always know. Or, as in her father's case, perhaps don't know they know.

My daughters have started telling me that I stare. This is a change, I think, which is why they bring it up. For most of my life I've been a listener. At least in the beginning, I think the reason I listened so intently was to have a chance of hearing the train before it ran over me.

Later I learned there were stories in people's everyday conversations, and if you intended to be a storyteller you had to listen. Sometimes the stories were about other people they knew, or had heard about, friends of friends. But most of the stories, even about friends of friends, were mostly about themselves, some aspect of them, some hope or fear or unspoken longing. That's where characters come from.

So I listened. I listened as carefully as I could even when I appeared to be going about my own business. I listened so hard that my head ached from the dense overlay of voices.

For a long time I couldn't bring myself to look

at their faces, afraid they would catch me listening. But the older I got and the more I wrote, the less I cared about what they thought of me. And I started watching their faces as they told their tales.

I've watched Melanie in just this way, as she's told her stories, thousands of times.

At times it has seemed as if my eyes have grown progressively wider over the years. I do stare, sometimes, I know, to the discomfort of others. I imagine that if I just look closely enough I will see the faces behind the faces of those speaking the words. I will see the characters themselves, struggling for recognition.

I want to see where the thresholds are. I want to know in which direction the doors swing. I want to know what lies outside the windows. I want to avoid the sharp corners where two or sometimes three walls meet. I want to figure out that convoluted floor plan before the days become too short and the nights too sweet.

I want to know where all my children live.

Christopher, our eldest child, is homeless.

I don't mean that he sleeps on the street, under a bridge, in a doorway redolent with piss and semen—though for all I know he has. It wouldn't surprise me to learn that he has gone hungry, panhandled, looted garbage cans, fought someone for a piece of bread or an inch of vodka in the bottom of a broken bottle, but that's not what I mean, either.

I mean he is without a home in the world. Without a place. Despite our fierce efforts and love that learned to be tough in every sense of the word, Chris does not seem to have a sense of his place in this life.

He also doesn't seem to have a sense of his own story. His pain, rather than providing any sort of energy or inspiration, has fossilized and been buried. Years of addictions have layered over it, turning it into a trick rather than a metaphor. Chris doesn't imagine; he lies.

Ten years old when he came to us, Chris almost let himself imagine us as his family. Right away he called us Dad and Mom. When the judge pronounced the adoption final, he squeezed Melanie's hand under the table.

But he's never quite been brave enough to take that imaginative leap. If you listed the things that happened to him before he became our son, they wouldn't seem as horrible as what happened to some of our other children who have much less trouble finding their way in the world. Most likely he wasn't sexually abused, for instance, or nearly killed. But, like the rest of them, he was abandoned again and again by adults he'd been persuaded to trust, had every reason to trust, and it was too much for him. He can't imagine a family. He can't imagine a place. He can't tell his story without lying. He puts all his energy into making a place for himself, and he's an alien everywhere.

No matter how hard I listen to my son Chris, no matter how closely I watch his face as he tells story after story that is not his, I have no idea who he is or where he lives.

Both Melanie and I grew up in green-and-gray rural places. I was raised in a small town in the Appalachian mountains of southwest Virginia, Melanie on the outskirts of an only slightly larger northwestern Pennsylvania town (also in Appalachia, a later and somewhat startling geographic discovery). Our roots are there.

Together we've always lived in north Denver,

the second-oldest suburb of this brown-and-blue city, on a street that can get busy at rush hour and when there's a Broncos game but otherwise doesn't make much commotion. We've put down roots here, too.

I was never very good with either my hands or feet. It always seemed to me they'd just been stuck on as an afterthought during my making. Dreams didn't translate through sports, or music, dancing, carpentry, plumbing. I was the bookish kid, more at home in the pages of a fantasy than in the room in the town on the planet.

But the need to *make* persisted. Books and puppets and games and, finally, pictures came to house my imaginings, making new spaces in the world.

In the countless crannies of the big old house we'd bought, our daughter Veronica couldn't find the exact space to fit the person she was becoming. She needed to be away from us and still close, separate and connected, still at home but at the very top of the house getting ready to climb out and fly away. None of us could have articulated much of that at the time, but the attic seemed to be the place.

There was evidence that the attic had been finished in the past, but it wasn't finished now. Nails, with fragments of black wood attached, dotted the roof beams. Remnants of antique electrical cable dangled between rafters. Off in the shadows, wedged against unused chimneys and jammed tight under the eaves, were a dozen or so sets of tarnished bed springs, a rusted sink or two, a few lost toys. In summer the attic smelled oddly sweet and comforting, like cookies baking.

I wondered why the rooms once up here would have been torn out. The house was full of mysteries like that—the back of a storage closet walled up to create a completely enclosed space, arcane electrical boxes, a stockpile of doors that fit no doorways we could find, sink fittings inside a staircase landing. Evidence of places created by those who had lived in our house, imagined and re-imagined to suit the tastes of the time and the individual.

There was no indication that the builders of any of these spaces had been professionals. I began to consider: would I do any worse than they had?

I did what I always do when I encounter something I don't understand very well: I read up on it. Mounds of books accumulated, on carpentry and electrical work and the joys and pitfalls of remodeling. I became an ardent fan of *This Old House*. Slowly, awkwardly, I began the process of creating for my daughter a space in the world, or at least a space in the house, with built-in drawers for the new outfits I would never approve of, bookcases to hold her soap opera magazines and true crime books I wasn't sure she should be reading, a built-in desk, even a built-in bed. And a secret compartment under the desk for hiding away from—or for entertaining, making peace with—any serial killers or white-gowned knife-wielding ladies who might drop in for tea and cookies.

"She's going to love this room," Melanie told me, quick to find inspiration in any household event. And she made sure our daughter knew how much work I was putting into making things as right for her as an amateur could.

I don't know if Veronica ever loved it. The sloping walls met at eccentric angles, and the wallpaper constantly defeated me. But I think she got the point. Her dad believed she had a right to her own place in the world, and would do whatever he could to give her one. Then it was up to her to make it work.

Since then I've made many spaces in our house: erected walls and reshaped ceilings, wired dark corners for light, put up bookshelves everywhere, teased all sorts of reading nooks out of random emptiness or random clutter (I love reading nooks, whether anyone ever sits and reads in them or not). I've changed the way air moves through our home, altered the way shadows lie. Though I still make no claims for myself as architect or craftsman, I've proceeded as if I knew what I was doing.

I've read that the aesthetic challenge of building something out West is competing with all that sky. Everything you lay against it seems unnecessary, if not pointless. Most buildings here keep a pretty low profile, seemingly more at ease in relation to each other than against the blue.

When a big one finally does go up, new buildings appear to take that pioneer as their backdrop, and eventually the architects seem to ignore the sky. At times it seems a race to see how quickly they can fill in the skyline and the last clear view of the mountains.

Among my personal favorites are the ones that go straight up and then add pilasters and broken pediments across the top two stories. It's interesting to imagine temples rising above the waters after some cataclysmic Colorado flood.

I suppose a major function of shelter is that it hides you. When I was a kid I found nothing more comforting than the inside of a cardboard box. If I really had to have a window I could cut the one I wanted, to see only what I wanted. The thing about the outside world is that somehow, eventually, it eats you.

Chris, my son, has found no shelter, no place to hide. Everything he's tried has only exposed him more.

I concede that everything eventually gets eaten. But I also believe that the spaces we make are still there, even after the house falls down. The room I made for my daughter could very well last as long as the Pyramids. Not the physical walls or the things built into them or the peach-blossom wallpaper, but the space. That imagined place.

I have not been able to make a space for Chris.

As I was finishing up the reconfiguration of the attic space, I'd gleefully inform Melanie on at least a weekly basis: "This is the last 2x4 I will ever buy." "This is the last sheet of drywall I'll ever carry." "This is the last bookcase this house can hold." Our house was finished and full.

Ah, but there are always repairs, responding to the wear and tear of occupying the place we've made. Maintenance. Stewardship. The shower's dripping. A pane in the bay window is cracked. The porch light's out again.

Creating a place is exhilarating, like falling in love. Maintaining it is pretty much endless.

I know it isn't practical, it doesn't light the room or plug the draft, but these days I spend most of my time with stories: reading them, making them up, listening to other people tell them.

At a block party a few years after we'd settled in here, a lifelong neighborhood resident told me a story about our house. Once upon a time, a husband and wife lived here, not very friendly, kept to themselves, and another person (male or female; child of the older couple or cousin, uncle, sibling; old or young—details unavailable) who was never seen, who lived in an attic room painted completely—including the windows—black. The neighbor knew some of this because he'd seen the family bring someone in and out under cover of night. And he'd seen the black room after the family had moved out. But like good storytellers everywhere, he didn't speculate much on what it all meant.

Thinking about the bits of black-painted wallboard I'd had to remove before beginning my daughter's room, I was glad for several reasons that I hadn't heard about this before. I don't know if I could have put my daughter's room into that same space once occupied by the black room. I would always wonder what it might do to her dreams.

Sometimes I wake up in rooms that haven't been built yet, or will never be built. Sometimes I wake up alone and understand that from here on out the faces I see in every window will be unrecognizable to me. But the world's colors are the same colors they have always been. And the spaces between the colors create a universal rhythm and language that all of us can understand.

So, as terrified as I am, I know this one huge house we all live in has always been pretty much the same. We just arrange it differently according to our personal tastes and the things that have happened to us.

But that's not much comfort when you wake up in the middle of the night and there's no one to tell you where the light switch is. When you wake up in what seems to be some stranger's house but is in fact your own personal and private dwelling, far removed from the house you've shared with your family for years. You can't find your way to the window. You can't even find your way to the bathroom. What is this place and how did I get here?

Many years ago, in our backyard, near the green apple tree, a few feet from the black iron fence, a new room began to take shape. At first no more than a vague geometric notion, it grew and spread until it evolved into an invisible house overlapping our house, sharing a few features with it: a daughter's bedroom, a corner of the basement, the south wall of the garage. Most of the walls in the invisible house, however, didn't match up with any walls at this particular Denver address; most of the invisible doors and windows led to spaces and vistas none of us had ever known.

At times I was acutely aware that this was happening, could see these other doors, smell these other walls. I think maybe the rest of the family knew it, too, although they probably would have described it differently. How could they not have known? After all, this was the place where we were all living.

Over time I realized that the room I saw when I opened my son Joe's door was not the same room he escaped to every afternoon for sleep and dream. And my daughter's room had far more complications in its wallpaper than I could ever see. Each of us lived in a different house, and sometimes those houses weren't even in the same neighborhood.

I don't think Chris has a house. I wish I'd known how to make him one, or how to teach him to make one for himself.

The other day a cab driver told me you have to position yourself to be available for miracles. There was only the most minimal context for this remark; he must have been driving around town with it on the tip of his tongue. It burst out of him as we rounded a corner and arrived at our destination, so there was no chance to find out more, but I bet there's a story in that, and probably someday I'll write it. You have to position yourself to be available for stories, too, and every encounter with every story is a miracle.

I wish I could help Chris find his story. I would position myself to be available for it. I would listen with all my heart.

Every night I climb the three flights of stairs from my basement office suite (a rather grandiose term for that rabbit warren stuffed with books, videos, computers, puppets) to the attic rooms it took me years to complete. What awaits me there is about as mundane as you can get: a stationary bike.

"It'll make you feel better," they tell me, but that isn't really my reason. "You'll look better," about which I no longer care. "You'll live longer," seems closer to my own motivation; I have children and grandchildren now, and I'd like to live long enough to hear as many of their stories as possible.

My favorite thing, the best thing I know to do

now that my body is older and fatter and gravity has become an invisible enemy I must fight just to move through the day, is to shut off all these attic lights I so carefully placed and wired, so that it's pitch black in the crown of our home, but even that isn't dark enough so I close my eyes as I continue to pedal, wheels slicing the air below me, invisible rooms rearranging themselves around me, and I rise through the roof of our house, settling on the roof line, exposed to the night and everything in the spaces beyond, while I continue to pedal.

One night I saw Chris there. When I first caught sight of the darkly coruscating shape, I thought it was a bird, bound as surely as the rest of us by gravity and need no matter how much we wingless creatures want to make it a symbol of freedom. A night bird, limned in moonlight, migrating somewhere or coming to roost in our house, a bird of prey or just a traveler through the dark. Sound of feathers.

Then I saw that its form was human, not avian, and even though I don't believe in such things I thought: *ghost, angel.*

I thought: *Lost child.*

I thought: *Chris. My son.*

He settled on another of the many roof lines of our house, out of my reach but close enough that it seemed plausible he'd intended us to meet up here, in this place as much in the high air as on the uppermost limit of the house.

"Chris?"

"Dad."

Exposed like a decoy, I was uneasy, even afraid, and glad we were encountering each other away from the rest of the family, who presumably lay below us safe and unaware. I don't think Chris would intentionally hurt us. But I can't be sure he would intentionally *not* hurt us, either. It's a terrible thing to be even a little afraid of your own child.

He said, "I have something to tell you."

I wanted to say, "Don't tell me That." I wanted to say, "I don't want to hear it." I wanted to say, "I've already heard enough of your stories, and I never know what's true."

Instead, I found myself assuming the listening posture I'd perfected over all those years, from which I could watch his face as he talked. The lower lip that still pouts when he doesn't get his way. The high cheekbones that give striking contour to his naturally round face and accentuate its gauntness when he's been shooting heroin for a while. The teardrop tattoo below his left eye.

He was crouching gargoyle-like on the steeply-pitched roof, and I was afraid for him. It's also a terrible thing to be afraid *for* your child, and it's part of the parental condition. For some of my kids I'm afraid they'll get hurt in love or won't find fulfilling careers or will let their talents go to waste. My fears for this one are considerably more primal: that he'll destroy himself and leave a trail of harm where he's passed through the world.

I could have just descended into the house again and gone to bed, leaving him out there to do whatever he was going to do, to tell whatever tales he came up with this time. Instead, I said, "I'm listening, son." And I was, with all my heart.

He said, "You know that time I ran away from that detention center when I was, what, fifteen? That whole summer? I hid out in this house. You didn't know that, did you?"

Actually, after he'd been captured elsewhere, we

had found evidence of his squatting. In the dusty, cobwebby space around the furnace, which we grandiosely call the furnace "room" because it has four walls and a door that closes (and because we like the idea of "rooms"), Chris had set up a place for himself, with a folding chair, a twelve-inch black-and-white TV that hardly could be said to work, a sleeping bag and pillow, upturned boxes for tables. All these furnishings he'd purloined from closets and shelves elsewhere in the house, and we'd never missed them. Dishes, too, and food—we found orange peels, a half-empty box of cornflakes. We also found potato chip bags, empty beer bottles, and cigarette butts, which he had to have brought in from outside.

While both of us are more than a little territorial, I'm usually touchier than Melanie about violations of the personal space defined by our house. But she'd been especially creeped out by the thought of Chris hiding in our basement—apparently for some time, judging by the den he'd made for himself—without our ever knowing he was there. "How could we not know?" she kept demanding, as if I could explain it to her, as if somehow there shouldn't be secrets about children and intimate places.

"I heard you," Chris told me now. He was dangling his feet over the edge of the roof like a little kid.

But then I saw him shoot up. Just like that, talking to me in the middle of the night while we both sat on the roof of our house, he injected something into a vein on the inside of his elbow. He made no sound when the needle went in. I thought I was going to be sick.

After a long moment, he went on. "All of you. I heard you walking around and sliding chairs and flushing and taking showers and laughing and yelling at each other and answering the phone and leaving and coming home and feeding the dog and doing laundry and cooking. I heard what you said."

"What?" I breathed. "What did we say?"

"Oh, just shit like how Veronica was never going to learn to make change and how some neighbor lady yelled at Anthony for singing."

My heart seized, the way it still does sometimes when an event is mentioned that occurred during that tiny but infinite period we had Anthony as our son. I said, "She makes change just fine now."

"And shit about writing. Lots of shit about writing."

"No doubt."

"And you and Mom were always saying you loved each other. Every day. All the time."

I was a little embarrassed. "Well, that's true. We do love each other all the time."

He stood up precipitously. By then he must have been seriously high. I wondered if I could catch him when he fell. I'd never been able to catch him, but maybe, somehow, this time would be different. He was tall against the night sky. A plane passed behind him, too high to hear, red lights in formation. "You guys never said anything about me."

This angered me. Melanie's always going on about respecting other people's perspectives. To hell with that. "Chris, that is simply not true."

I saw something in his hand. A weapon? But it was a piece of the roof he'd pulled off or found already loose, and I imagined him tearing the house apart under us, shingle by shingle, brick by brick. Whatever it was, he flung it into the air, and it vanished; I didn't hear it hit the ground. "Never once. Nobody mentioned my name. Like I didn't exist in this—house." I knew "family" was the word he'd intended but hadn't been able to bring himself to say.

My legs were cramping. I stood up, too, and swayed dangerously, flailed for something to hold onto, found a cable I hoped was the telephone line and not a hot wire. "We talked about you a lot while you were missing." With silly fastidiousness, I corrected myself. "While we thought you were missing. Missing to us, anyway. In fact, we had to make a rule that we'd talk about something else. We just kept going over and over the same things. Maybe you were dead. Maybe you were going to be okay. Your mother was frantic, and you know how she is when she gets like that. She *talks*."

We both chuckled, and I was shocked to realize we were sharing a father-son moment of exasperated fondness for a woman we both loved. Then Chris slid on his heels down the peak, sending up sparkling debris, and I thought for sure he was about to fall or jump or otherwise take flight. He came to a stop at the very edge. "What about you? Dad?"

"What about me?" I dissembled, knowing full well what he was getting at. He just snorted, and after a long pause with him on the edge of the roof, I felt compelled to tell the truth. "You're never far from my thoughts, Chris. I don't know how to think about you, but I think about you a lot. I always have, ever since you've been my son." I swallowed, closed my eyes, held on tight to the cable as vertigo welled up, and made myself add, truthfully, "I always will."

"So how come I didn't hear you?" he whispered.

"I don't know. But it's true."

"How come I don't know that?" he shrieked, and flew away.

When the kids are all grown and gone, with luck to places of their own and not just away from this one, will we still live here? Will this old house be too big for just the two of us? Will there be too many stairs, too many rooms, too many stories or not enough?

When one of us is left alone, will the widowed one hide in this house, in a smaller and smaller space, with only the man on the ceiling for company?

Neighborhood kids, including our own, try to make this a haunted house. Generations of neighborhood kids, probably, so that it's become the stuff of legend.

It offends Melanie that people want to think of this house as haunted. But she also knows that her experience of it as friendly and warm is equally self-indulgent. It's inherently none of those things. It can be any of them, whatever you need it to be. It takes what comes. It houses both life and death, as well it should. Anthony's life and death here have hallowed it. It provides a place for whatever happens. We need places like this. It's why we need places—for things to happen in.

The fact that some people thought our house was haunted actually surprised me at first, and now I'm not sure why. When we moved in, it certainly looked the part. The vine covering about half the south wall was in one of its periods of

aggressive growth, obscuring the roofline, hanging from the porch ceiling like a dead woman's
hair, invading the bay window casings, destroying
portions of crown molding, fascia, Dutch gutters.
Rotten patches of bead board allowed the vine
access to the attic, and during rare but occasionally intense rainstorms, water poured in through
the cracks. All this wood trim was painted a dirty
gray. The screens in the high dormers were dark,
torn, rusted.

Scary enough for a house at street level, but this
one crowned a ten-foot hill, so you had to look way
up at it as you approached or passed by on your
bike or glanced back over your shoulder. A veri-
table jungle had grown up around it, junipers and
Siberian elms and ragweed and Canadian thistles
over and around the wrought-iron fence.

The first few Halloweens we'd open the front
gates as far as they would go and light the house
and porch with as much welcoming illumination
as we could manage. Then I'd watch as cos-
tumed children large and small stopped at the
front steps and peered up, considered, decided it
wasn't worth it, and scurried on. No doubt some

of them had been told about the strange family with the unseen inhabitant in the black attic room. No doubt some of them feared the ghosts of the Dobermans who used to live here in the yard and leap out from the dark places. You could watch them making up legends if they didn't know any: A lady in white with a knife and no voice stands by people's beds at night. Or there was a corpse buried in the basement, blood stains under seven layers of old wallpaper.

And, I finally realized, no doubt some of them knew our son had died here.

A house like ours calls for stories. Maybe all houses do. We do our best to answer that call.

The only time this "haunting" upset me was right after my son died. Anxiety then was like a horse I got on every night when I went to bed, riding me into dark and incomprehensible places I'd never imagined. When I'd finally fall asleep for two or three hours, it would be out of exhaustion from the trip. After eight years of this, a kindly doctor talked me out of my aversion to medicines and gave me the pills that would put a stop to these nightly rides. By then, however, I'd started losing people's names, and I haven't yet found all of them.

I suppose some places and people, victimized by unfortunate beginnings or bad memories, are more likely than others to be thought of as haunted. It's hard to change the reputation once it's grabbed hold. Ask any ex-con. Ask Chris.

For myself, I've always been skeptical. Not that I don't believe there are things out there beyond our understanding—I'm convinced that's always the case, part of the real world we must all contend with. But I don't trust the conventional language for these experiences. It's the words I doubt. I suspect the best way to describe a mystery is to let the imagination do its job—which is to say, make something up.

And lately I've come to believe in something other than haunted places we visit out of curiosity, too much time on our hands, and a desire for a good story. I've come to believe there are places and spaces that haunt, that travel with us wherever we go.

I know people who will live only in houses where no one else has ever lived. It's like when your mother told you to take that spoon or pencil or blade of grass out of your mouth because you didn't know where it had been. Or like the sects that counsel their members against garage sales because previous owners might have been in the service of the devil and the objects consequently possessed. I doubt I have the right words (or just the plain right) to convince them that everything we have has been someplace else, everything is borrowed, stolen, or inherited for our safekeeping and stewardship. Everything is possessed.

I admit to having lots of fears for my wife, my children, my grandchildren. Not too many for myself anymore. Fear of embarrassment, so strong throughout my childhood and adolescence, certainly seems to have faded, or else I couldn't say the things I'm saying to you now.

I do fear I'm going to be one of those old men who'll say damn near anything, which could be a bit of a burden for those who love me. Sometimes I fear it may go further than that, and they'll have a certifiably crazy patriarch to manage (not that patriarchy is ever known for its sanity or manageability).

Before the end of his life, Melanie's father lost her name. Veronica is afraid I'll lose hers someday. I'm tempted to tell her I don't entirely trust names anyway. Instead, I make the dishonest promise that I'll always know her name.

Perhaps when I'm old I won't talk about anything but the places that visit me for brief moments at a time. Places I've been, and places I've never seen before. Another fear I'll share: what if I decide to stay in one of those places forever?

* * ✯ * *

The first place I lived in was a small house in a small town a few miles from the even smaller Appalachian village I would come to know as my home town.

I've seen three photographs from the first house: one of the front, one of the back with me in the strangest little walker/tricycle combo, and one of me standing in my crib beneath a picture of the White Rabbit from Alice in Wonderland—her guide, you may remember, into another place. Only three photos, and I was barely two when we left that house forever. Yet, on a visit home from college I amazed my mother by drawing an accurate floor plan of my first home, complete with placement of the furniture.

Now, I'm a skeptic. Maybe my youthful conviction that my drawing was precisely accurate simply overpowered my mother's uncertain memory. I do have both a vivid memory and a vivid imagination.

But in the invisible house we live in, the house that overlaps and shares features with this physical structure sitting on this hill and then goes far beyond it, I know where the furniture goes even though its appearance changes every time I look at it. One room holds a cabinet-style phonograph and a box full of the shards of my mother's records I've broken. In another room I find my first tricycle buried under huge black chunks of coal. One door is the door to what I dreamed last night, which I must never open again. Another is the door to nowhere.

The invisible rooms of old furniture are not what really interest me. Sometimes in the middle of the night when I'm walking through them, I find myself muttering, "Been there, done that," over and over like a protective chant. Truly interesting are the invisible rooms I've never been in, in whose tall crystalline mirrors I catch glimpses of myself doing things I've never done. I worry that I might not be able to visit all the rooms in the invisible house in whatever time I have left to me.

I haven't been back to my hometown in many years. For someone whose mind travels great distances in the average day—and whose relationship with daily practicalities no doubt suffers for it—I'm a fussy and reluctant traveler through the physical world. I just don't want to go anywhere (England, for some reason, is a notable exception). I prefer to spend my time here, in this place which is home, the first place in my memory that has truly felt like home. I have children and grandchildren who came to life for me here. And a son who died in this house.

Anyway, I don't need to travel. Other places have a way of traveling to me. Particularly when Melanie is away, I find myself waking up in rooms other than the one I went to bed in. I wouldn't want to overstate the phenomenon—it isn't a sustained hallucination of any sort. The experience lasts only moments, but it is as vivid as the taste of today's lunch in my mouth. I see the shadows made by an old mobile on a yellowed ceiling I haven't slept under in thirty years. I smell the flowers and hear the buzzing of yellow jackets in a bush on the other side of a screen that rotted out during my teens. My first gaze of the morning is at a multi-colored horizon of book spines in that crowded twenty-five-dollar-a-month college apartment.

A different but related experience happens to me late at night. Somehow the gravity of the world shifts around me in the darkness and I know the walls have changed to those of some other place even though I can't see them. They're closer to me than they should be, or much farther apart.

I don't find all this particularly strange. I just have a vivid imagination and a vivid memory and sometimes they're the same thing. Certainly there's room enough for both before breakfast.

* * ★ * *

An uninhabited house offends the natural order. The whole point of a house, its reason for being, is to provide shelter to human beings, who can't live long without it. A vacant house begs to be filled, with new owners, with squatters, with ghosts, with fictional characters (maybe even a man on the ceiling) who can be whatever the house needs them to be. Filled, inhabited, or razed.

* * ★ * *

Sometimes I get lost.

That's not the most eloquent way I might have expressed it, but it's the simple truth of it. Sometimes I get lost. Melanie tells me again and again how solid I am, how responsible, how adult. Much to my own surprise and certainly despite myself, I do seem somehow to have achieved those conditions. There's not much choice, really, if you have children.

But even with that, sometimes I get lost. I don't really think I'm more delusional than your average human being, but sometimes I go walking in these rooms for hours, even days at a time, and I don't always know which room I've settled in for this particular portion of the evening. I don't really know who'll be sitting in that armchair. There are moments I can't remember who is alive and who is dead.

When did we paint the walls that color? It

may have been decades ago. It may have been tomorrow.

How old are my granddaughters? Where is Chris? What did I miss? Do you know what hour is sunset this evening? And what about tomorrow's sunrise? I don't want to miss it. I don't want to miss anything. But sometimes it takes so long to go through all these rooms. And the children who play here won't always give me their names. Give me a call and we'll have dinner together sometime. Just give me a call. Give me a call.

Sometimes I think getting lost is my one true talent, the thing I've always been best at, the thing I will be remembered for. Getting lost and finding my way back. Finding my place. And knowing all along that eventually there will come a day when I won't find my place, I won't find my way through this ever-complicating home that has claimed me all these years. I won't find my way out. And that'll be. That'll be. Lost in my place. Forever in my place.

5
NAMING NAMES

"What's that boy's name?!"

That's our granddaughter Katy, four years old. Her favorite punctuation is the question mark combined with the exclamation point, whose name I've lately learned to my delight is "interrobang."

Katy likes to keep her characters straight. To do that, she requires names.

"Baba?!" That's her name for me, a linguistic example of phylogeny recapitulating ontogeny, the individual replication of the evolution of the species. "Baba" actually means "Grandmother" in many parts of Eastern Europe, including the region now once again called Slovakia where my not-very-distant ancestors came from. Not being Slovak, Katy wouldn't have known that when in some way she decided the name for who I am to her would be Baba. When she slips and calls me Grandma, I object. Stubbornly, even petulantly, I won't answer to that name from her, though it's a precious and well-used name in its own right.

"Baba?! Baba?! What's his name?!"

I tell her again, but it obviously doesn't satisfy her. Thumb in her mouth, eyes wide, she intently regards our friend, whom she's met before. She wants to know about him. The name is a start, but it's not enough. She wants to know who he *is*, and, of course, I can't tell her that.

But I understand what she's asking. Once I've found the right name for a character, I can write his or her story. Every character in the world is waiting to be named, and every character resists naming.

"Baba?! Baba?! Baba?!" Katy is nothing if not persistent. "What's your friend's name?! What's his name?!"

I remember the very moment Katy finally understood who Steve was. "Papa," she said, and kissed his hand.

Sometimes Steve has a harder time than Katy keeping his characters straight. His memory for other details—the location of our first dinner date, for example, including the exact table where we sat—is encyclopedic, but a while ago, after a decade's lost sleep, he began losing names. Names of movie stars and politicians and writers. Names of people to whom he'd just been introduced and names of people he had known for years.

I know it worries him. But so many names pass through our lives, and they change so often, who could be expected to remember them all?

The round-faced five-year-old with the Prince Valiant haircut and huge green eyes was our daughter. Sometimes I could not fathom this miracle. Sometimes I still can't. And yet, being my children's mother, being Gabriella's mother, has always seemed utterly natural.

For one thing, I love her name. If I'd had naming rights I might well have chosen it. On her original birth certificate it was spelled wrong, "Gabrilla" without the "e," not corresponding to the way she and, presumably, her birth parents pronounced it, sounding like the evil stepsister. This felt to me like another manifestation of how profoundly they neglected her. *Hey, it's reprehensible enough that you fractured your child's—my child's—skull and exposed her to sex at such an early age that she'll never have*

the words to tell about it; for God's sake, couldn't you
at least get her name right? The name you gave her?
That beautiful name?

On this summer evening, Gabriella was drawing. Sunshine through the prism in the kitchen
window made rainbows on her shoulder and sleek
hair. Stronger than my strong desire to hold her—
to breathe in her presence in my life, to absorb
through my pores who she was and would be to
me—was my resolve not to be a distraction.

She'd started with the big rough shape of a
green heart—green, not red, an aberration from
which I was eager to infer courage and creativity.
Whether by design or lack thereof, she'd left plenty
of space between its wobbly curves and point and
the four edges of the paper.

I offered no comment, tried not to steal too
many glances, not to put my own names on what
she was doing. She had to be free to see for herself
where the heart would lead.

But I couldn't help passing closer to her than
absolutely necessary on my dinner-making
crisscrosses of the kitchen, couldn't quite resist
the desire to be at least a witness. This is one

of the countless dilemmas of parenthood: when to stay out of their way, when to stand close by, whether it's permissible to appropriate just a little for oneself.

Carrying a pan from the cabinet to the stove by way of the table, I glimpsed four appendages on the bottom of the heart, two on either side of the point, the purple pair on the left smaller than the brown pair on the right. Feet? I knew not to ask.

When I looked again, under cover of getting out the big cutting board I could have done without, she had drawn a fat blue wiggly line all the way around the outside edge of the paper and was starting around a second time. A frame, I thought, until I saw that it was attached to the heart down near the point. A tail? In some places it veered inward a little, and in others it left the paper altogether.

The meal was ready before my daughter was. Hoping the rest of the family wouldn't complain too much about the delay, I put the food in covered serving dishes in a warm oven and busied myself loading the dishwasher which ran almost constantly in those days, sweeping the floor that always needed sweeping, adding to the endless grocery list. Lopsided yellow ovals appeared, one in each hump of the heart, and a spray of rainbow lines on either side of a big pink dot.

Then, abruptly, Gabriella put her crayons down. "Mommy," she said, and the name for our relationship thrilled me. As it still does. "Mommy, look."

Invited, I sat down beside her and took the drawing she pushed across the table toward me. "Wow," I breathed. "Gabriella, this is beautiful."

She nodded, gave me a quick hug, and squirmed down off the chair.

In an attempt to capture the moment—whose nature, like the nature of all moments, was fluid—I said quickly, "It's a beautiful heart."

She was already on her way out of the room to find her brother to play. I was about to tell her they had to come to dinner instead when she looked at me sharply and declared, "It's a cat." Because she was the artist, "cat" was its name.

I said, "A cat shaped like a heart. Or a heart shaped like a cat." Because I was the viewer and therefore part of the act of creation, because reality occurs at the place where horizons fuse, those were its names, too.

Ever since we've known her, Gabriella has shown artistic talent and a personal vision of the world. Her father and I have done everything we could think of to nurture and support her. In point of fact, we've done more than she has; Gabriella's artistic nature has become, in some distressing and fundamental way, more ours than hers.

When she was six, she won a children's art contest, saw her painting displayed at a local store. As a teenager, she had a show of her odd and fascinating little sculptures, where half a dozen sold. Rather than encouraging her, these successes and our enthusiastic pride seemed to scare her. She hardly works with clay at all anymore, and her rare paintings tend to be cursory and tentative—though once in a while she'll come up with something brilliant, that talent and vision of hers spurting out despite all her considerable efforts to keep them down.

One of the names Steve and I have had for Gabriella is "artist." It has not turned out to be a name she has for herself.

I was making my late-night paternal rounds to check on the kids—those I could still check on, those I still might help—the children still alive and out of prison and not yet moved away. Or out among the crowds of children lining the sides of the road in my imagination.

I eased open the door to Joe's room. Even before my eyes registered the empty pile of blankets, I could tell by the quality of the silence that he wasn't in his bed.

Not so much ignoring as disregarding the anxiety that comes naturally since Anthony died, I stepped in and shut the door. Joe's room smelled of the white cat who despises everybody but him, the young-guy piles of unwashed clothes, the chemicals from the photography hobby that gives him and the rest of us such pleasure but remains—well, undeveloped. Cool air and the city-night light seeped in from the wide-open street-side window, and for a moment I thought he'd run away.

But there he was, sitting in his window, one

foot braced on the porch roof and the other dangling inside his room. If he knew I was there he didn't acknowledge me, and I didn't immediately announce my presence.

I wanted to say, "Be careful, just be careful."

I wanted to say, "You're not spying on people with those binoculars are you?" and, "Go to bed. It's a school night."

I wanted to say, "Tell me how the world is from where you sit."

But more than anything else, I wanted to say, by not saying anything, "Go where you need to go, son. Do what you need to do. Use this house, this room, this window as your lighthouse. It's home base. Venture out as far as you like—you can always come back here in the end."

Not much given to talking about such things, Joe would, I knew, recoil from such verbosity. He'd laugh to hide his embarrassment, although he does permit a kiss on the cheek from his dad now and then. For myself, I was torn between the confusing obligations of fatherhood and the sense of a delicate magic surrounding moments such as these. I stood in the shadows and watched my son, his profile against the blue-black patch of sky, his wiry forearm languidly braced against the window frame. I assured myself that I was close enough to catch him if he fell (and isn't it ridiculous, the power we believe we have to protect our children!), but otherwise I'd stay out of his way.

Melanie tells about the moment she understood that Joe was no longer a child. She says they were sitting on the living room couch talking about something serious in Joe's life, and all of a sudden the realization came upon her fully-formed: *Now I have a teenage son.* Something about his posture, the shape of his face, the lines of his body—something she was certain had not been there the day or the moment before.

For me, it's been gradual and incremental, as much a process of layering as of emergence. More than with any of our other children, in Joe I can see the child he had been still playing in his face, in his voice, climbing in and out of the spaces between his ribs. On this night, the adolescent perched in the window was clearly the six-year-old I'd first met and the young man he is today. Beyond that—the thirty-year-old, the eighty-year-old—I don't dare but can't help imagine, and they're there, too, in the boy on the windowsill.

Up here in this thick-walled and foliage-wrapped house, we're often unaware of what goes on in the neighborhood, especially at night. It's usually trouble, so we're just as glad to have slept through it, although the feeling of isolation and the false sense of peace can be disconcerting. Sometimes we find out the next morning or weeks later: Another fender bender at the corner. Cars vandalized up and down the street. The big Siberian elm at the other end of the alley split in two by lightning. A coyote strolling big as life along our decidedly urban sidewalk. The man on the ceiling swinging from one ceiling to the next to the next; the neighbors never say a thing about him because they don't and don't want to know each other anywhere near that well. When Joe was younger he was most often the one to bring us the news, for Joe knew everybody and they trusted him enough to tell him things, but if they ever mentioned some fear they might have, some emotional difficulty, he didn't pass that information along to us, for Joe has never been one to talk about such things.

The drama unfolding outside and below my son's room was well within my field of vision. No doubt Joe was seeing it better than I was, though, since he had the binoculars. I wondered what the old man who is the watchman of the neighborhood, walking the block several times a day to see what's going on, would have to say about this in the morning.

Joe swung his other leg over the windowsill *(be careful!)* so he could look straight down on the scene below. Now his back was to me. I couldn't tell if he knew I was there, and I decided, for no good reason, that it was up to him to notice and acknowledge my presence, not up to me to announce myself.

In our front yard stood three adults, one I thought I recognized and two I'd never seen before, and two children who were intimate strangers to me. The boy, who looked to be about six, was telling everybody what to do. "Gabby," he directed the little girl, "you go stand there."

She said his name in that round two-syllable protest exactly like the first time we heard her on the phone, but she did what he said. In those days she pretty much always did what he said. That didn't last.

To the woman with the stocking cap and bad teeth, the boy commanded, "You sit there." When she didn't move fast enough to suit him, he balled his fists and stomped his feet and repeated the instructions more imperiously, and he added a name that shocked me, though I supposed it shouldn't. "Mom! What did I say? You sit *there*, right this minute!"

Laughing self-consciously, tears in her eyes, she went and sat on the couch where he was pointing. The small boy stood still for about ten seconds, which was as long as he ever stood still, then turned his skipping, jumping attention to the man who in body type looked so much like him and in face not at all. My throat tightened. "Dad," said the little boy outside, and I put my hand on the shoulder of the teenager who was *my* son even though the child had not been, and my son Joe gave my hand a quick, surreptitious pat. "Dad," said the child to the man with the knife, "you sit there."

"Who you think you are, boy, tellin' me what to do?"

The man advanced on the boy, and I stepped forward into the window. As if I could do something about what was happening, what had happened many years before. Nobody in the scene below looked up. Nobody, including the boy, knew yet that we were there. They would, though.

The child planted his feet in a cocky fighting stance and crossed his arms over his small chest. "Sit by her," he ordered. "You have to sit by her."

"What? Why should I do that?"

"Because I said so."

Still the man didn't obey, and I held my breath to see what this brave boy who would soon be my son would do next. There was a long, tense, showdown sort of pause.

Then, still brandishing his knife, the man swore and strode across the grass-and-gravel space meant to suggest a visiting room, a one-way observation mirror no doubt hidden behind the vine, and slouched onto the couch not exactly beside his wife but on the same piece of furniture.

The child was wound very tight. In him I could see the hours-long rages that would erupt from Joe after he became our son, when he would flail and sob and scream, blacken Melanie's eye not out of any meanness but because the fury had to go somewhere, and we held on held on held on and assured him again and again that he wasn't going anywhere and we weren't going anywhere and we would get through this together because that's what families were for.

The boy was yelling now. "Hold hands!"

The other woman in the room, the social worker, shook her head and smiled sadly. "The Little General," she murmured, the name Joe had earned around the agency. And it wasn't a name that would have embarrassed him, because it was, quite simply, the name for what he needed to be. For years he would wear a variety of "army" pants and camouflage gear, embarrassing his sisters who didn't want to be seen with him. But he had no self-consciousness about it. I envied him, my son.

The man and the woman had made no move to touch each other. "I said hold hands!" the child shrieked, and threw something at them, a handful of something, dirt or gravel. They looked at each other and at the social worker, who nodded. They grasped each other's hands, but it looked more like a gesture of aggression than a caress.

"Okay!" the boy shouted, beside himself now, jumping up and down and kicking the furniture and throwing everything he could get his hands on. "Okay, okay, okay! Now, you tell us good-bye!"

The process of separating children from adults who are capable of giving life but not of nurturing it often involves a goodbye visit during which they admit to some of their errors and give the children permission to go on with their lives. Its formal structure is designed to protect the child's often raw emotions. For the adults it's a final chance "to do the right thing" by their children. For the children—well, I can't pretend to know what my children, all five of my children, must have felt at such an odd sort of ceremony. And watching this tableau on our front lawn didn't help me. All I could see was that this little boy was the clearest, the most self-assured person in the room. I was amazed. I would have been terrified.

I didn't know what to say to him about that time in his life that he didn't, clearly, already know. At the end I kissed him on the cheek and, like generations of southern men before, called my son "honey," and that kiss and that name are things I still give Joe today, and they are gifts the grown-up, highly reticent Joe still accepts.

Shape-shifters and dreamers and singers of songs. Sometimes we are cats. Sometimes we are hearts. How strange it is to dream of childhood and wake up an adult, to realize the names that populate our consciousness now—including our own—will one day be names from the past.

How strange it is to be someone in the mind and someone else in the mirror. If we could just imagine that other self well enough, our physical form might change forever. If we changed the furniture would we be different people? What if we moved to another city? What if we shaved, lost weight, ate our vegetables, drank more coffee, took up golf?

★ ⋆ ★ ★

In the narrow space between first word and complex sentences, our oldest granddaughter Christiana invented a game. "Grandma Melanie," she'd insist, which was a lot to say for someone just learning the multiplicity of the language.

Christiana has more grandmas and great-grandmas than the average child. At least one of them has abandoned her, perhaps two. Out of the common human impulse to name the order of the world—even when the order is painful, even when it is false—she said to me once, "I guess that's what grandmas do. They go away." I protested vehemently, took her face in my hands, pointed out that I'm still here.

I did not promise, have never promised anybody, that I won't ever leave her, because, of course, one way or another I will: either I will die first or she will. Now that she's older, Christiana thinks about that, too. But in the meantime, it's important that she differentiate one grandma from another.

"Grandma Melanie. Say the pictures."

With her in my arms I'd make my way slowly along the upstairs hallway where family photos are displayed. "That's you when you were a baby," I'd tell her. "That's your daddy when he was little. That's your cousin Katy."

"That's my cousin Katy. One time she ate a bee."

"That's your Uncle Anthony."

"He died, huh?"

"That's right. And here's your great-grandma, my mom. She died, too, before you were born."

Concepts like "died" and "before you were born" are hard for a two-year-old to grasp, but Christiana kept going into the mystery, naming her characters. "Grandma Melanie, say the pictures."

"That's me with my best friend when we were in high school."

"That's Aunty Gabby, huh? That's Uncle Joe, huh? That's you, huh? That's me."

Saying the pictures. Giving her characters names and stories, and herself a place among them, a place in the gallery of our house.

When we gave the man on the ceiling a name we took a first step toward controlling the influence he had over our lives. Knowing the power of names, writers will sometimes spend months searching for the right name for a character so they can properly tell that character's story. As writers, Steve and I sometimes are able to root out our own personal demons, chase them down, and pin names to their backs. If the name fits well enough you can almost see the demon diminishing before your very eyes: Rumpelstiltskins struggling and withering where they've been fixed inside the display case of story.

During the last summer of his life, my father said a car waited in the woods for him, covered by underbrush, camouflaged by trees.

Can't you just see it? A humped shape that could be anything, but is, specifically, a car waiting specifically for him. He'd see the car, if seeing is what it was, and his slipping gaze would light on it. His face would light up.

But by then his fear had come to feel to me like curiosity, and maybe I didn't understand that he was afraid. Or maybe he was, in fact, curious.

That last fall, my father said he had one foot in another world already. And smiled. But maybe by then the rage he'd promised ("If I ever get senile, I'll shoot myself.") had disguised itself as serenity, and I didn't understand how angry he was. Or maybe he was serene.

My father forgot my name but still knew I was his daughter. Then he forgot I was his child and that he'd even had a child, but still knew I was someone important. Then he didn't know I was there at all. But, for the first time since he'd been seven years old and his mother had died and they'd said don't cry you're a man don't cry and he hadn't, he spoke—repeated, perseverated, because he'd forget he'd just said it, and every time it gave him such new pleasure—he spoke of love. Of love, flat-out, no codes or disguises, naming it.

Christiana, Katy, Mya, and Sophia, the great-granddaughters my father never knew, also live in this interior space. It's not impossible that he met them there, playing in the brush-covered car.

Christiana would have regarded him impassively. "Impassive" is one of the things she does best, along with "silly" and "pensive" "I know who you are," she might have announced. "I said your picture."

As long as this great-grandfather of hers kept his distance, Mya would have allowed herself to be interested, especially if he sat in that humped car in the woods. But if he'd approached her, she'd have tensed. If he'd tried to take her in his arms, she would have honked the horn.

The baby Sophia, having more recently than the

rest of us been in the world that car came from, might just have been able to focus on him for a second or two before something else in this world caught her attention.

From a step or two away, Katy would have taken him in. She'd have pointed with all four fingers of the hand whose thumb would have been in her mouth (which, she will tell you forthrightly, is for the purpose of keeping her safe) and would have demanded again to know: "What's that boy's name?! What's his name?!"

6
ELEPHANT SOUP

Not very obsessively but with small, solid pleasure, Steve and I collect storyteller dolls. An icon from the Southwest United States, storyteller dolls are really sculptures, sometimes plain terra cotta or whitewashed white, but usually brightly painted, most commonly palm-sized but occasionally as tiny as the tip of a thumb and once in a great while as massive as boulders.

There's always an adult with mouth and eyes wide open. There are always children, clambering, playing, cuddling, listening attentively with miniature hands in miniature laps.

Sometimes they are specific, with detailed costumes and well-defined facial expressions, the faces of the attached children individualized. Sometimes the children's faces so mirror the storyteller's that the narrative they're all engaged in seems to be one of those we necessarily tell ourselves generation to generation. Sometimes all the faces are blank.

The price of a storyteller doll varies depending on size, intricacy of detail, and, tellingly, the number of children. In a sense, too, the price varies according to the story being told.

Do the children have a part in creating the stories for the storyteller to tell them? If a tree grows in the forest and there's no one to tell its story, can it be said to grow? For that matter, can it be called a tree?

Such questions have to do with the nature of the language we use to symbolize a thing, not with the thing itself. At least, that's true about trees. A tree wouldn't be called a tree—wouldn't be called anything—without human words, but it doesn't depend for its existence upon human perception of it. I'm not so sure about stories.

Some stories we tell ourselves "for our own good." We tell them to our children, who are apt to call them "lectures"—their word for the unnecessary and irrelevant. In response we are apt to rename them "under-appreciated." I imagine the stories told by storyteller dolls to be neither unnecessary nor under-appreciated.

In more abstract versions of the dolls, the children's heads are like growths on the storyteller's body, great or tiny distortions of flesh, mutated receptors directly connected to nerves and bloodstream. The storyteller's mouth is like a yawning wound letting loose a necessary howl from that dark country just the other side of flesh. The storyteller doesn't particularly want to tell the story, but is compelled to do so. The children would rather be playing, but their horizons have fused with the teller of the tale.

We tell stories because we need to, and because our children need us to. I think I was a storyteller long before I was a mother. I think I tell stories because of all the relationships in my life—because I was a child of my particular parents, because of how I see, because of other lives that swirl and eddy through mine. Because of Steve. And, of course, because of my children.

My parents had put together for me little set pieces out of their lives, which they recited in the same way every time so as to gather the power of refrain or ritual or magic spell. I believe now that the stories had been selected and edited, all but deliberately, to illuminate and to limit illumination. I think both of them yearned to be known, especially by me, their only child, and both were horrified by the prospect. So they put forth truncated and stylized narratives that required me to meet them more than halfway. I have not always been willing to do so, but I am now.

The stories were selected and arranged by theme, and the themes of my parents' lives were remarkably similar. Each, for instance, had a single innocent, amusing tale with sinister undertones: the knob on the tree that the child who would be my mother routinely scared herself into thinking could be somebody lurking; the rich golfer offering to "adopt" the teenage caddy who would be my father. Each had one coming-of-age tale: my mother's first job away from home in the big city; my father's cross-country Depression-era trek in search of work; these were synopses without supporting detail, so my imagination doesn't have enough to go on.

Each had a litany about the death of a young mother, language become meta-language that took the story deeper and also kept it distant:

"I was seven years old when my mother died. They told me, 'Big boys don't cry,' and I didn't. I didn't cry."

"The doctors told my mother to drink cow's blood and eat raw liver, but she couldn't do it, and so she died."

There were three or four stories apiece about a wicked stepmother and a younger sibling singled out for particular abuse. Throughout the years each made recurrent mention of one and only one childhood friend. The story of how they met was always collaborative, my mother's part the romantic frame, my father's the gentle jokes.

All my life I have worked to know my parents better (except for those periods when I wished I didn't know them at all). Most of the time self-referentially, sometimes even wanting to understand them other than in reference to myself, I have searched and struggled and fought and waited, and I've come up with ways of thinking about them that may or may not be factually true. Truth, like creation, seems to me to take place at the intersection between sender and receiver.

So I say about my parents that each of them

loved five people throughout the eighty years of their lives: their mothers, their fathers, their little sisters, each other. And me. For their other siblings they nurtured disdain unleavened by anything I would call love or even filial affection. Their friendships were not allowed to take deep root. They did not claim their grandchildren.

For many years I chafed at, mocked, resented, wrote about how constricted they were, how inaccessible, their inability or unwillingness to take even the most minimal emotional risk. Until it dawned on me that loving the five of us could be cast as an enormous risk, a breathtaking act of courage. This framing device, this change of genre or shift in point of view, allows for quite a different story, using the same facts to arrive at a different and no more or less truthful truth.

Framing has to do with what we make things mean. This is a story I often tell about Steve:

The Elephant's Ear

The storyteller watched all the children cuddling in his lap and climbing on his back, but he was especially alert to the wan, fragile little girl crouching on the kitchen chair. He took a calculated risk. "You know what that soup's made of, don't you?"

Having learned to expect treachery and horror from the world at large, not knowing yet what to expect from him, she stared at him, spoon halfway to her mouth. "What?"

"Elephants."

"What?!"

"Yep." He nodded solemnly, continuing to eat his cream of mushroom soup. "Elephants."

"Huh-uh." Now she was staring at the lumpy gray liquid in her bowl, eager to play this game with him, not sure it was a game, thinking those *could* be pieces of elephant in there.

"Yes," he persisted, straight-faced, vigilant so he could gauge how far to take the fancy. Playing like this, he could sometimes make her laugh, a rare and breathtaking sound, but if he went just a little too far she'd dissolve in tears and he'd feel as if he'd harmed her, as if the play had turned into abuse and the fantasy into a lie. "See? Right there, that's part of the elephant's ear."

Later, Veronica would tell her father that elephant soup was one of the ways she'd learned to trust.

Later, he'd watch her imagination develop into a sudden intense love of reading, a quick wit and enjoyment of word play, a childlike but not childish engagement with her own daughter in conversations with imaginary friends and scenes of elaborate role assignments ("I'm the Mommy, you're the baby! I'm the girl, you're the puppy! I'm the vampire-slayer, you're the vampire! Okay?!"). Observing how healing this was for her, he'd allow himself a small, careful satisfaction that he'd given it to her, and she would understand the gift and be grateful and know to pass it on.

But at the time he first told her about elephant soup, she was seven years old, and he was newly her father, and adults had done worse to her than feed her chopped-up elephants, and she didn't know what to make of it. She took another spoonful, saw for herself the lumps that *could* be pieces of tail and trunk and Dumbo ears, made a face and dumped it back into the bowl. If it was mushroom soup, she might like it. If it was elephant soup, she didn't dare eat it. A cautious child by nature and circumstance, she opted for self-protection over this particular form of sustenance and pushed the bowl away.

Later she'd insist that the elephant story had ruined mushrooms for her forever. A small price to pay, if you ask me, even if it were true. We all knew there were other reasons she came to hate mushrooms, such as the hormonal changes of pregnancy that made them and a host of other foods nauseating. But this was her contribution to the elephant soup story, the way she collaborated to construct a family legend.

And, of course, it's absolutely true.

Daughter of the daughter who consumed the story about elephant soup, Katy is a born storyteller. Long before anyone could understand her, she had joined the oral tradition: telling stories, acting them out, snatching pieces from the big mysterious world and spinning them into her own truth to bridge and interpret and expand, discovering and rediscovering how reality puddles, the fundamental process of creation happening before our eyes.

The moment she could talk she was interrogating and exclaiming. In one tale, "Shark?" and "Fish!" and "Water?!" were the only intelligible words, but she used her whole self to embody the narrative. In bright pink pants and a lacy shirt, wild blonde hair in the dapple of spring leaves, she plunged as if underwater, feinted, swam, gasped for air, kicked to get away, dived deeper. Enthralled, we followed her. We had a pretty good idea what she meant. When she seemed to have reached the end of the story, we applauded, often prematurely, for there is always more to tell.

Did we, in fact, know what she meant? Was the story we made up for ourselves, out of the cues she gave us and those we added on our own, the story she had in mind? Was my story the same as Steve's, the same as her mother's? Was she the storyteller or the child sitting at the storyteller's feet? Are we?

"Omigod!" Her eyes are wide, her hand over her mouth. She stands motionless in the middle of the room; she is not often motionless. "Omigod!

There's two of you! And two of me!" She begins to back away.

A chill runs through me. I think of childhood schizophrenia; this is an occupational hazard of my work with the families of disturbed kids. She does not appear to be playing. I say her name and "What do you mean?" in a clumsy attempt to bring her back to reality if, indeed, she's escaped it.

"Oh! My! God!"

She is utterly convincing. This is making me nervous.

Then she shrieks with laughter and darts away yelling, "Don't chase me! Don't chase me, Baba!" which means I'm supposed to chase her. When I catch her under the dining room table she throws her arms around my neck and we giggle together, transported. Later her mother assures me that "Omigod! There are two of you and two of me!" is dialogue from an Olson twins movie. I'm relieved, bemused by my own credulity, and thrilled by this child's willingness to enter fully into Story.

What I'm about to do, a season or so later, is a risk. But she's been talking about death for months, asking what it means, worrying that she'll die and, worse, that Mommy will, just having encountered the fact of mortality and struggling to come to terms with it for the first of what undoubtedly will be many times in her life. So when she asks, "Can I see her?! Can I hold her?!" I glance at her mother, who nods tearfully, and I bring in the body of the yellow cat Cinnabar who'd been in our family twenty-two years, almost as long as our family has existed in any form at all.

Our eldest son Chris saw her born. Ten years old, he'd just come to us, having taken "you can't trust anybody" as the theme for his life story, he would teeter for many years on the bridge between anger and love. Being present at the kittens' birth didn't work a miracle, but I think Cinnabar was a constant for him, an emblem of "family," less demanding than the constancy of his dad and me, a story in its own right and a metaphor he was free to accept or reject.

That, of course, is my story of my son and Cinnabar, not his. I hear him tell his own children, "I've known Cinnabar all her life. I saw her born." That's all he ever says.

Cinnabar gave us many stories. I doubt she

intended to. She was a cat. Whatever storytelling might go on in the feline sensorium, I'm not species-centric enough to imagine it's humanoid. Her gifts to us are *our* stories, and as long as we remember that, they're absolutely true.

Cinnabar used to lie on our bed in a golden pool. Our youngest child Gabriella couldn't leave her alone. She'd poke at her. She'd tug at her tail. She'd put her nose to Cinnabar's nose, blow on Cinnabar's whiskers, brush her fur backward. We warned her. With small growls and hisses, tail twitching and stalking away, Cinnabar warned her. The little girl persisted, perhaps exploring power, respect, alien sensitivity, the place where stories are born at the intersection of one life with another. Or perhaps just being stubborn.

Whatever the impulse, she wouldn't stop pestering the cat, and one day Cinnabar had had enough. Quickly and cleanly, she stuck a single claw into each of Gabriella's tender temples, just as cleanly withdrew them. As if she knew this was a young one who needed at the same time to be taught a lesson and to be protected, she didn't go for the eyes, didn't scratch, didn't even draw blood.

But our daughter got the message. Shocked and tearful but not really hurt, she backed off, and she took the first step that day toward learning how to be with Cinnabar on Cinnabar's terms.

At Cinnabar's grave, our daughter, tall and beautiful now and insightful when she allows herself to be, delivered the eulogy, her story of the story of this beloved animal: "She was a good kitty. She taught me an important lesson."

I'm not sure Gabriella actually remembers Cinnabar's teaching. But her dad and I have told the story so many times it's become her story, too, more textured and resonant for having been passed along.

"Why is she so cold?! Why is she so—"

"Stiff," supplies the child's mother, who has loved this cat as long as she's been our daughter.

"Why is she so stiff?!" The small hand lifts the paw and lets it fall. It moves like something inanimate. It is something inanimate.

"That's what death is, honey. She's not in her body anymore."

"Where is she?!" A reasonable question.

"I don't know. Nobody knows."

"Can I see her face?!" The pink towel is pulled down, revealing the sweet, stiff, furred face, slitted yellow eyes, pink nose. The child gasps but does not turn away, knows to go forward into her sorrow. "Can I hold her?!"

When she sits on the couch to receive the slight body, her feet stick straight out the way her mother's used to. Struck by gratitude and loss and the accumulated power of repeated patterns, I am aware of stories passed down through generations. A story is being passed down right here and now.

I put the swaddled body into her arms. She cradles it, not the way she might cradle a doll or a baby brother or a living pet but exactly as she would cradle a loved, dead creature. "Can she feel me pet her?!"

"No. She can't feel anything anymore."

"Why?!"

"Because she's dead."

"Why she's dead?!"

I take a deep, ragged breath. "Because everything that lives has to die."

"Why everything that lives has to die?"

"I don't know."

"Will you die, Baba?"

"Yes."

"Will I die?"

"Yes."

"Will Mommy die?"

I meet her gaze and tell her the truth. "Yes."

She opens her mouth, throws back her head, wails. I stroke her hair, but I don't tell her to stop crying or that everything's all right. Her mother doesn't, either, though it costs her. After a few moments the child's anguish subsides, and she takes one hand away from the cat's body to tug at my fingers. "Sit here by me!" Crying now, I sit where she tells me to sit. Her mother stands beside her, crying. She looks from one of us to the other, alarmed but not in the panic that usually strikes her when her mother cries. "Why everybody's crying?!"

"Because that's what we do when we love someone and they die. We're sad, and we miss them, and we cry."

"I'm crying!"

"Yes."

"I wish Cinnabar didn't die!"

"I know. I wish she didn't die, too."

"I wish she didn't die!"

"I know."

Sobbing, head bent close over the body across her lap, red-gold hair brushing Cinnabar's red-gold fur. "But I love her so much!"

And there it is, the understory, source of horror and romance and suspense and mystery and science fiction and fantasy, the reason we keep writing and reading about death: I love her so much! I wish she didn't die! But she dies anyway.

After a while, when the time seems right, I say, "I'm going to take Cinnabar's body back outside now, honey. You need to say good-bye to her."

Without hesitation, joining herself fully with this story, she keens, "Good-bye, Cinnabar! Good-bye!" and lets the body go.

Later she will take me aside and confide, "Baba! I really, really, really understand 'die'!"

When I relate this story to someone who wasn't there, someone who doesn't know this child, I'm compelled to add the ironic comment, "If that's so, she's a better woman than I am." But I know what she means. Or, what she means when she says "I understand" intersects somewhere with what I mean when I say, "I understand," and together we have a story.

Stories are masks of God.

That's a story, too, of course. I made it up, in collaboration with Joseph Campbell and Scheherazade, Jesus and the Buddha and the Brothers Grimm.

Stories show us how to bear the unbearable, approach the unapproachable, conceive the inconceivable. Stories provide meaning, texture, layers and layers of truth.

Stories can also trivialize. Offered indelicately, taken too literally, stories become reductionist tools, rendering things neat and therefore false. Even as we must revere and cherish the masks we variously create, Campbell reminds us, we must not mistake the masks of God for God.

So it seems to me that one of the most vital things we can teach our children is how to be storytellers. How to tell stories that are rigorously, insistently, beautifully true. And how to believe them.

7
TELLING TALES

When I was a boy I had no way to tell my stories, or at least no audience I judged as safe. But I told them anyway. I lied. I learned to make stuff up. I had always been a storyteller with an audience of one, telling myself tales as far back as I could remember. I used them to explain myself to myself. I used them to find my way through a world I could not even begin to understand. I used them to describe the mysteries around me. I used them to create a future for myself, when I did not really believe I had a future.

Having children someday did not figure into any of these tales. Here my much-vaunted imagination met its match. I could not imagine myself in any real relationship, much less a relationship with children. I'd have been thrilled to foresee that one day I would use Story to explain the world to my own children, but it was not an idea I could entertain at the time.

Instead I made up stories about why I was who I did not want to be:

HIDEOUT

Above the garden was a place that scared me. It was wild, like a set piece out of one of those Tarzan movies where natives were pulled off the path by things that lived underneath. I wasn't supposed to go there. "You stay outta there, boy, you hear me?" My father would be furious. Sometimes I wondered if this choked, overgrown place was my father's hideout, and what I ought to be afraid of was stumbling on him hiding out there. I was twelve, too old to be afraid of such things and too young not to be.

And so, of course, I couldn't for the life of me stay away. I raced my bike past the overgrown lot, feeling—though I didn't know the old story then—like the boy Gautama passing the dark wood. Nothing jumped out at me with sticky claws, and my father didn't find out, though our house as usual felt on the verge of bursting into flame.

The next day I stopped on the road and waited. I held my breath, let it out in a whistle, hummed that stupid country tune that was on the radio all the time and I couldn't get out of my head. To give the impression I couldn't care less, I busied myself with a low front tire, a loose shoelace. But whatever was in the woods was better at this couldn't-care-less business than I would ever be. It wasn't going to come out. I would have to go in.

I didn't know what to do about my bike. Left along the side of the road, it might be a clue for a search party if I disappeared, which was a good thing. But it would also tip off my father. For four days I rode past, hoping a plan would occur to me, hoping the woods themselves or whatever was hiding in them would decide for me. Finally, I walked the bike a little way off the road, laid it down, camouflaged it with branches and brush, and, feeling mournful and guilty, left it there while I went on in.

There was something exciting and disturbing about the fact that it wasn't really a woods but a town lot allowed to run wild. The pale, ringed cuts of the upended trees were human-made, smooth ones by a person with a chainsaw, jagged ones by a person with an axe. The brush hadn't piled up like that by itself, had been purposely cleared and collected. I found no actual footprints, but a sort of path that had to have been made by feet that must have been human.

I followed the path. The light in here was gray-green. On the road behind me cars went by, not enough to be called traffic but reminding me both that I wasn't alone and that I hadn't escaped. An airplane buzzed overhead and from habit I looked up, though the tree canopy and the cloud cover meant I had no hope of seeing either the plane or its trail. Something that could have been either a bird or a squirrel chittered. Vines snaked around my ankles, reminding me to keep an eye out for snakes, but I didn't see any. Off to my right was a bush with red berries that might be poisonous. Off to my left was a hut, mounded with kudzu that had been cut back for a window and a door. Inside the hut was a boy about my own age, sitting cross-legged on the dirt floor.

"Hey. You're trespassing."

"Says who?"

"Says me. This is our property."

"Oh, yeah? So?"

"So where do you come from?"

There was no answer. To fill the silence, I pointed toward the farms back over the hill where I'd explored despite Dad's inexplicable rules. The boy just grinned.

"You new around here? I've never seen you in school." To be honest, I didn't pay much attention to any of the kids in school. If I didn't look at them, maybe they wouldn't look at me.

The boy didn't confirm or deny anything. Over the next week or so, we didn't tell each other our names, but we played Tarzan and Jungle Jim and Robinson Crusoe—the boy was darker than any other kid in town and volunteered for the "native" parts, once the story had been explained to him, particularly the reason his name was "Friday."

Mostly we played Pirates. The boy claimed to be a "Chinee" Pirate, which was pretty exotic. "Hey, we could be professional pirates when we grow up."

"How would we do that?"

"If you stay a pirate until you're an adult, that automatically makes you a professional."

"Huh?"

"Well, maybe I can't do that. But I bet you could."

"I don't know about that," the other boy protested, but with a dreamy smile.

Almost right away, I started feeling sorry for the boy in the hut. He was always there, waiting, as if he didn't have anyplace else to go. He was always wearing the same torn and dirty blue-and-yellow-striped shirt and brown shorts and holey sneakers with no socks. Maybe his parents didn't care about him or maybe they just weren't strict, or maybe he didn't have parents, which would be a great mystery.

"Don't let my dad find you."

"Why not?"

"He hates Jews. He had this officer in the Navy."

"Yeah? So?"

"That's all he's ever said about the war. Oh, and one time his ship was hit by a kamikaze and afterwards he found his friend's arm all bloody and with the watch still attached."

"Wow." After a momentary silence to appreciate

this horror in the edgy prurient way of twelve-year-old boys, he demanded, "What makes you think I'm a Jew?"

I said, not entirely to the point, "He doesn't know what to make of negroes."

"Make?"

"No telling what he'd do with a Chinee pirate. Probably call the sheriff. Maybe I could vouch for you."

"What's 'vouch'?"

"I don't know."

"Well, maybe you could."

I started sneaking food to the boy in the hut; there was always plenty of leftover fried chicken in the refrigerator.

Clothes would have been too obvious; my mother would have noticed when she did the wash. Besides, I had the feeling if I pushed too hard the boy would leave and maybe not come back. I so much didn't want that to happen.

But one day it happened anyway, of course. On my way to school I stopped to give the boy in the hut one of the Karo-syrup-on-white-bread sandwiches our mother put in our lunches that nobody would trade for, and the hut was so empty it almost wasn't a hut anymore, except for a couple of the boy's comic books I would hide away in secret places in my various rooms for years. They would somehow vanish, and I would forget their titles. For the rest of my life I would sorely wish I still had them.

My parents' stories about their own lives were fragmentary, plots truncated, motivations unclear. Melanie describes much the same experience with the stories her own parents allowed her about their lives.

Both our mothers had many suitors. My father once rode a motorcycle into a relative's living room. When another boyfriend tried to talk my mother out of marrying my father, her defense was that the wedding invitations had already been printed. My father spent their wedding night drinking; my mother spent it weeping.

"So why did you do that?" I'd ask. "Then what happened?" They'd just shake their heads, or tell me they didn't know, or ignore the question altogether.

Melanie says she didn't ask about motivation or what came next. She just took everything in and, when she got past the need to spurn it all, she filled in the gaps.

So we were both invited—compelled—to make stuff up out of our own imaginations and our observations of the world. This, of course, is where the act of creation happens, at this juncture of experience and imagination; it may be where reality happens, too. Many of the bits we invented seemed highly unlikely, but the details were nice:

Melanie's mother frequented a candy store on the corner. At various times her favorite candies were licorice, peppermints, and nonpareils.

My mother once had a hat of rose-colored silk. When sunshine filtered through it in a certain way, her face glowed.

Melanie's father once wrote a long poem about God, with precise if occasionally strained rhyme and rhythm. He worked on it for months. When it was finished, it pleased him. He shredded it and scattered the pieces like ashes into the Monongahela River.

My father had a hideout back in a hollow, a green and private place with trees. He stopped going there at about the same time he started drinking, when he was much too young.

Now I'm at an age when I wonder what my kids and grandkids will remember about me. What stories will they come away with after I've thrown all this material at them?

"He sang silly songs in the car."

"He put on a maroon velvet wizard's cap and he had something he called a magic wand and he exorcised the monsters from under my bed."

"When he was a kid he had an imaginary friend who lived in a hut in the woods. I don't know why he did that. I don't know what happened next. Did he ever tell you what happened next?"

We each have our own stories to tell. My children's stories—even their stories about me—are not my stories, and my stories—even about them—are not theirs. I try to remember that when, despite or because of all the love we have for each other, our lives begin to separate.

Stalked By God

One night when he was ten years old, he saw God. Worse, God saw him.

Over the course of a single week when he was ten years old, he saw God.

Since he was ten years old and saw a face in the clouds—silver hair, flowing beard, eyes so full of rage he thought he might burst into flame; your basic Old Testament God, because that's all he knew—since then, he has seen faces in everything.

The moon in southwest Virginia is sometimes as big as ten houses and ripe enough to fall. This night, when he was ten years old, complicated black clouds hung in front of the moon, letting light out in slivers and crescents. The face they revealed was dark and brooding and angry, unquestionably God's face. A faint breeze animated the face just enough to show him it was real.

When he couldn't take it anymore, he went inside and hid in his bed. Bad enough that the face of God had been there and he'd been the only one able to see it—far worse that God had noticed him.

The next morning, passing by the neighbors' house as he did every day, he saw a face in the screen door. He stared at it, realized it must be some sort of shadow cast by someone standing a foot or so back, politely said, "Hello."

No response. He walked closer and saw that it was a pattern in the screen, as if someone had stood there looking out for so many years the oils in his skin had discolored the mesh in a pattern to match his face. The thing seemed pretty improbable but it also felt scientific, so he decided to go with it.

Later that day, around sunset, he was looking at a tree in the side yard when suddenly, with a shock, he was seeing thousands of small faces etched into the bark. They all had reddish eyes and pink halos around jaws and cheeks. The tree crawled with their anger. Suddenly he knew all these little faces were about to start singing, and if he heard their song he would never be able to get it out of his head. He got away from there as fast as he could.

That night as he was washing up for bed, he saw faces in the translucent patterned marbling on the pale green bathroom tile. Hundreds and hundreds of faces.

In the mirror the next morning he found faces in his own face, dozens of faces in the creases of his skin, surrounding the moles, tucked up onto his eyelids.

This went on for days. He found faces in the wallpaper, in the grain of the wood floors, in the rugs, in the soap scum near one corner of the sink, woven into every bedspread in the house.

He became convinced that the only possible explanation for all these faces was an answer to his other major question of the time: what happens to us when we die? The world couldn't just forget all about us, could it? It had to have a way of making a physical remembrance, a memorial, so it must have a way of taking pictures, but maybe they were more than pictures, maybe the images were ever so slightly alive. Maybe they were aware.

He worked out this cosmology in some detail. The faces shrank and the awareness diminished as time wore on. So the face in the screen was someone who had died very recently, and the tiny faces in the tree were ancient, the spark beginning to leave them, and maybe that was why they became so angry when they saw him.

And the faces in the tile had been gone so long they probably had no spark left. To see them was like looking at skeletons.

"You're getting to be such a big boy. Too big now to sleep in the same bed with your brothers."

"Why?"

"You sleep in here now."

"In the guest room?"

"You sleep in here. But you keep all your toys and clothes and things in your brothers' room, okay?"

"Why?"

"Because this is the guest room."

"But we never have guests."

"Never can tell. You sleep in here now but it's not your room. It's the guest room. You're getting to be such a big boy."

Always afraid of the dark, even on the hottest summer nights needing protective strata of sheet and blanket and quilt, now he stayed awake all night trying to interpret the familiar and alien noises that filtered through from both outside and inside. In his blood, in the air moving through his body, were voices and almost voices, no words, a beautiful abstract vocal music immobilizing him with anxiety. Maybe these were the voices of the dead. Maybe that's where you went after you died, into other people's blood, other people's lungs. And that's where you lived until everything everywhere ended. Hands over ears, he listened to the voices in his blood, until he couldn't stand it anymore and pulled his hands away, which meant that now he had to listen to the wind's monologue and the trees' conversation and the dark man at his window scratching and mumbling and scratching again.

Finally, in the middle of the night, he began screaming. His parents came. From the way they looked at him and asked questions, it was obvious he scared them a little. They thought he was screaming because of the wind and the branches against the window, and because there was something broken in him.

But he was screaming because he'd understood how alone he really was, and however much they might love him, it would never be enough.

However much he would one day love his children—and he would love them immeasurably—it would never be enough, either. That's another of the dilemmas inherent in parenthood: we are required to love our children in every conceivable and not-quite-conceivable way, without measure or limitation, and still it will never be enough.

Toward the end of my second short stay in a mental hospital—

Do you trust me enough now to believe what I have to say? Or has my credibility with you been destroyed by this disclosure that as a young man I took a break from college for a far more specialized education in one of the east coast's finest asylums?

Writers worry about credibility. But at this stage in my life I have other things to worry about.

Toward the end of my second incredibly brief stop in a rest home for weary mental travelers, my doctor told me I played the walk-on role of mental patient better than most. I think it was his way of saying it had been a useful part for a time, but now I needed to move on.

After I played the crazy guy, I played the quiet,

responsible guy. My reward for that performance was getting to play the husband, the father, and the seasoned storyteller. It's been a good run, and maybe those are the roles I'll end my career with.

Knowing I could play another role seems to give me the option not to. Writing the parts, as many as I can as fully-imagined as I can, lets me play them without losing myself in them.

These are the tales I tell myself about myself. Everything I'm telling you here is true.

SEE ME

"Company!"

That was the signal the three little boys had been waiting for. They sprang into action.

They stripped to their underwear. They hid, two behind doors at opposite ends of the living room and the other behind the edge of the archway to the dining room. They waited for the exact right moment.

The brothers had had plenty of time to practice their game. Company hardly ever came to their house. A few of their father's drinking buddies would come over, a neighbor or two now and then, and their grandparents, always looking profoundly uncomfortable, as if afraid they'd hear a story they'd rather not know. The boys' friends never came. The bear in the house kept them away. During the long summers, when there was no school, it was as if the family were a world unto itself.

In the fall, when schoolmates traded stories about the summer, the oldest brother couldn't tell that most of what happened every summer of his life happened in his head. He couldn't explain that the world he lived in shared only a few vague features with theirs. He didn't dare admit that his best friends had no more presence than a dark line of clouds in a swift-moving sky.

The company sat on the couch and the parents sat in the chairs and the four of them were telling stories. Despite or because of the dearth of books in the world they lived in—hardly any in their house, a single rack of paperbacks at the drugstore, no library in the whole county—the brothers were growing up immersed in stories. Their father gave them plenty of stories—often drunken and obscene, often violent, sometimes over-the-top emotionally. Everyone had a story to tell: about the Civil War battle nearby, about hermits and moonshine and incest.

Now the parents and the company were telling stories about how the old lady McGowan had passed on after suffering all those years, poor thing, and her children were squabbling over who got the sideboard that the boys' mom said was an antique and had been in the family for generations and their dad said—like he was enraged that the mom was so dumb—was just a piece of junk.

It was Saturday, so the dad had been drinking all day. The middle brother had found the bottle of Jim Beam right out in the open on the porch and emptied it into the toilet, risking but this time not incurring the bear-like wrath. As always, as if by black magic, another bottle had appeared, not to mention a case of Budweiser. It was Saturday, so the mother had been cleaning and cooking all day, and now she was all dressed up and fluttery as a chicken to have company in her house.

The oldest brother (author's note: that would be me) went first, just like they'd planned. The mom was passing around the tray of brownies and fancy white napkins when he stuck his spindly bare right leg out from behind the door and wiggled it a few times, shouting, "See me! See me!" The middle brother shot his spindly bare left arm into the open archway and waved the hand like Miss America, screeching, "See me! See me!"

The youngest brother, who always had to go last because he was the youngest, balanced on one foot and held onto the door jamb with one hand and did a crazy half-dance with his spindly bare other arm and leg and crowed, "See me! See me!"

The name of the game was "See Me!"

"See me! See me! See me!" they chorused, and then ran away on a river of giggles to hide in their room.

They couldn't hear the mom's words but they figured she was saying she was sorry and how embarrassed she was and she didn't know why her sons would behave like that. Probably she had tears in her eyes. They felt sort of bad. The dad growled, once again, that those boys were driving him crazy. This scared them, but it was probably the point of the game. There was never anything calm about the man. When the brothers really got to him, he had a face like a slavering cartoon bear. People were afraid of him. That's why company hardly ever came. That's why Mr. and Mrs. Glover left in a hurry. The brothers were afraid of him. "See Me!" was a way of calling out the monster, calling his attention to them just to see what would happen next.

"See me! See me! See me!" the little boys whispered to each other as the heavy unsteady footsteps came toward them down the hall.

The Day He Died

The day he died he was eight years old and something terrible happened that day but he's not sure what it was. He was too busy dying.

The day he died it was a hot summer day and nothing gloomy or sad about it, just hot, maybe a little too hot because his head was so full of the heat he couldn't think straight.

The day he died they all came and worked on him as if he were a car that had broken down and they were shouting and arguing and he was so embarrassed he wanted to apologize but could not speak.

The day he died was very much like the day he was born.

The day he died the insects all put on their secret ears and came right up to the door, listening.

The day he died the world finally showed the other colors it had been hiding from him.

The day he died there were new sounds in the air but nobody was applauding.

The day he died every dream he'd ever had turned itself inside out and emptied its pockets.

The day he died windows lost their transparency.

The day he died the floors rolled up into the corners.

The day he died the roofs flapped once, twice, and then were gone.

The day he died the doors broke out of their hinges and walked away.

The day he died all the telephones rang but there was no one on the other end of the line.

The day he died the pond froze over quietly with him inside.

The day he died he got out of his bed and climbed up the stairs. There were new windows on the second floor for him to look out of but it took all his strength to get them open. Finally he stuck his head out and looked around. Everybody he knew was out there going about his or her business but looking much older than just the day before. They all glanced up at him and smiled. Then the house turned and went into the bathroom, stood in front of the mirror. He could see the whole house now with him inside. He looked just like his father as he stood at the sink and washed his hands.

School's Out

It had been a day like any other. The paper boy had been late, and when he did arrive threw the bundle the size of a phone book so hard against the door one of the small bordering panes cracked down the middle. Next door the couple had fought for a while, driving the husband out to mow the lawn the third time that week.

Clouds drifted by, rapidly at first, then more slowly. In the trees the squirrels played their little tambourines.

It was the day he realized he had lost understanding. He still had the basics down well enough—he could understand simple sentences, if they did not involve issues of morality or existence. He could still drive his car, operate a garage door opener. He knew which end of the telephone to speak into, carefully selecting his words to avoid offense. He knew which end to hold to his ear and pretend to listen.

But he no longer understood why he did any of these things. He no longer understood why he even bothered. He did not understand why he got up in the morning. He did not understand why he was unable to sleep. He did not understand what everybody seemed to be trying to tell him. He simply did not get the secret message of the world. He simply did not know how other people saw him.

In the long afternoon of the world the cats rode their silver bicycles into the sunset. The cows whispered together of troubles in the pasture. His wife was leaving him, and now he did not understand if she'd ever loved him at all.

The list of all he had not understood as a child would have flowed out the door and down the sidewalk where pedestrians would have had good reason to fear their footing. He had not understood if he was loved; he had not understood if he was lovable; he had not understood if he was safe; he had not understood if he was normal; he had not understood if there was even the smallest place in this world for him.

As he grew older he had seemed to obtain a kind of beginning understanding. Yet now, as he was entering the final quarter of his life, he did not seem to understand anything.

Out on the lawn, the dogs played an awkward game of croquet. They had plenty of enthusiasm, but a poor understanding of the rules.

Not knowing what else he could do, he grabbed his lack of understanding and took it for a walk outside. The trees had begun their premature descent into the ground. Before disappearing completely, they were broad leafy bushes, contracting in their shyness. The birds circled overhead in confusion. The squirrels angrily packed up their instruments and headed west.

In his stroll through the long afternoon of the world, his lack of understanding sang of the joys of openness and flexibility. His lack of understanding grew wings and flew away.

He returned to his empty house and sat on the edge of his bed. His mouth tasted like tangerines. "School's out," he said to no one, as outside the houses disappeared one by one.

FINDING MELANIE

Wherever Steve went, whatever he did, he was looking for Melanie. Getting up in the morning—for a while not being sure whether he was awake or asleep, whether it was morning or afternoon or midnight, and seeing no reason to worry about the distinctions; listening to the creaks and cracks of his joints the way you'd listen to an old house settling even though it had been on the same site for a hundred years; sitting on the edge of the bed until his head cleared; fumbling for his slippers—he was looking for her. Reading the paper, he was looking for her. Walking around the block, chatting with neighbors, making soup, watching the six o'clock news. He was looking for Melanie, who'd left him after forty-eight years but could not be lost to him forever because he would not be able to live without her.

This lovely spring morning he'd decided to stay inside and conduct an organized search for her in the house. He didn't know why he hadn't thought of that before, and now it seemed obvious that she had to be in here somewhere. Where else would she be? Anticipating that it would take several days to find her in this big old place, too big for just the two of them and unthinkable for him alone, Steve whistled almost cheerfully as he brewed tea and worked out a plan.

He started in the basement. Getting down the stairs wasn't easy, and he tried not to think about climbing them again. For Melanie, he could do anything.

She wasn't in the laundry room, where detergent grit had caked on the inside edge of the washing machine lid and a white sock lay on the floor. Her sock. A gift from her. A sweet clue. After all these years, Melanie still gave him a pleasant little thrill.

She wasn't in the pantry. The cobwebby metal shelves were half-filled with cans and boxes and bags of foodstuffs. Steve pocketed three cans of chicken noodle soup, touched by how she took care of him. When one of them fell out and rolled, he didn't try to retrieve it.

She wasn't in his tool room. He didn't go past the doorway. She wasn't in the space behind the furnace where nothing worth storing was stored anymore. She wasn't waiting at the outside door that hadn't been opened in many years and might not even open anymore, might not even be a door. She wasn't anywhere in the basement. He hadn't thought she would be. But when you love somebody, you search everywhere.

When, sweating and groaning, he finally made it to the top of the stairs, he had to sit in the kitchen for a long time before he could go on with his search. Everything ached. Everything ached for Melanie. His heart wasn't beating right, maybe another heart attack, maybe just an old and damaged heart needing time to recover from exertion, but he knew what it really was: Melanie had left him and broken his heart.

He hoisted himself to his feet, collapsed back onto the chair, wished for his cane, yearned for Melanie. If he waited for the chest pain and shortness of breath to ease, he'd never find her. The bones of his skull creaked from the weight of the second floor above him and the attic above that. If he had to search up there to prove his love for her, he would. Again he pushed himself upright. Vertigo made everything shimmer dangerously. The need to find Melanie stayed steady.

He found her then, not ten feet away from him, doing dishes at the sink with her back turned. Thinking to kiss the nape of her neck, he took two, three, four steps toward her, and she was gone.

"Melanie."

He found her again in the dining room, watering her plants. She was beautiful among the sun-glossed leaves, and for a long moment Steve stood and watched her, leaning on the sideboard for balance. When he began to make his way around the table, intending to take her in his arms watering can and all, she was gone.

He found her again in the living room, slippered feet up on the hassock he'd made for her decades ago, lap full of embroidery. He started to kneel at her feet, which would have cost him plenty, but she was gone. He found her again in the front hall, putting on or taking off her blue coat, and he hurried to hold it for her for the pleasure of her body against his through the soft cloth, but she was gone. He found her in the leaded glass window beside the front door and his eyes filled to become prisms like the glass, but before his vision cleared she was gone.

Another painful climb for Melanie. Steve set his jaw, grasped the banister, pushed and pulled himself up to the landing. His need to stop and rest there was almost overwhelming, and Steve panicked. He had to find Melanie. Longing for Melanie made his heart hurt and his breath come short and shallow. Meaning to force his left foot onto the next step, he lost his balance and cried out. Welcoming the pain in his chest as her hand on his heart, as proof of his devotion and hers, Steve fell at last into the arms of his beloved.

TIDAL POOL

The tiny woman with the wild and brilliant white hair was all but swallowed by the massive wheelchair and all its electronics and accoutrements and appendages, but her eyes bright as slivers of mirror held no signs of distress. She rocketed the chair along, gunning for adventure, her grandchildren struggling to keep up.

"Baba Kate! No!" the small one insisted. "Is dangerous!"

Kate instantly wheeled around and circled shark-like, finally scooping up the giggling child. The child leaned over and whispered something into her grandmother's antique hearing aid.

The chair stopped itself as a woman in uniform strode in front of it and smiled. "Are you here for 'The Pool of Life?'"

Kate frowned. "Do they still really call it that?!

She never said anything without an exclamation point.

"Treacly, I know. But it's always been called that. And museums are, well, traditional." She gestured toward a hall leading off to the left. "You'd best hurry—no entrance after the show starts."

Kate's chair bucked and started up again. The little girl on her lap shrieked.

They took their positions around the ring encircling a huge metal bowl, at the bottom of which was set a gigantic plate whose painted electronics changed pattern as people moved their heads side to side. Once all the positions in their ring were occupied, the seats spread and locked. Kate's wheelchair was on a shimmering plate that held her firmly in place. Then this ring lifted and tilted to give the observers a better view of the floor of the bowl.

The little one cried because she wanted to sit in Baba's lap during the show until her older sister shushed her and held her hand.

Her baba said, "It's okay, sweetheart! You watch extra carefully in case I miss something! Then you can tell me a story about it later!"

Kate looked around as other rings rose, tilted, and locked. She smiled as the bells for each ring triggered randomly as they ended their final checks. There was a hush of anticipation. Even her grandkids were still, the little one with her thumb in her mouth peering down at the multi-colored disk. Then, "Oh, Baba, how pretty!" as the colors rose out of place and began to blend, blurred edges dissipating as a fluid climbed the walls. When it reached the level of the lowest ring where Kate and her grandchildren sat, it stopped. It shimmered, waves began to form which splashed to the edge with a yellow halo of spray. The younger children laughed and the oldest looked mortified when the youngest tried to touch the spray, exclaiming, "Hey!" as her hand halted at the invisible barrier.

Clouds formed above the fluid and lightning rang down from the ceiling far over their heads. The mist and fluid began to swirl, picking up speed until it looked like the side of a tornado.

Then, as quickly as it had begun, the swirling stopped, the lines of force broke apart and fell away. Inside the bowl there was now a primitive landscape: part of a volcano cut away so lava was visible bubbling upward, and great lizards, early dinosaurs, the narrator explained, and Kate thought what an obvious thing to say. Listening a bit longer and finding nothing more surprising, she decided to tune out the rest of the narrative; she didn't have time anymore for someone who couldn't tell a decent tale.

The fluid and the electrical storm came and went, and each time revealed a different scene to have emerged from this imaginary tidal pool. At one point the volcanoes erupted, sending great sparks and hurtling embers into the air, driving the children back into their chairs. "Baba, it scared me!" Kate responded with a pat and a smile.

She didn't fully understand the technology, even though she'd read everything she could before coming here. In all that mountain of material she hadn't found an explanation that satisfied her for how these flying reptiles could look directly at you and respond to how you looked and behaved, how the ancient people would answer questions, even sing songs or perform bits you requested.

Then the fluid was dropping once more, the haze dissipating rapidly into nothing, and there were the elephants floating out of the tidal pool, and all at once Kate was laughing and crying. Her grandchildren stared at her in alarm, until she shouted, "Soup! It's elephant soup!" They all laughed so hard everyone else thought them crazy, not knowing the story the great-great-grandfather had told Kate's mother when she was a little girl, so many years ago.

25 of the 487 Rules of Storytelling

1   If every word were tattooed into your skin,
    would it be a good fit?

2   Read aloud what you have written.
    Does this sound like you speaking?

3   Be generous with your characters.
    Life's hard enough.

4   Don't drive, or write, after ingesting drugs
    or alcohol. Don't drive or write when feeling
    too full of yourself.

5   Adherence to safety precautions and local
    ordinances is always recommended.

6   Don't let anyone ever tell you you have nothing important to say.

7   Tell a new story every day. Find an old story and put a new twist on it.

8   Make stuff up, but never lie.

9   Is that your face in the mirror? I don't think so.

10   Every family has its imaginary history. Fail to speak it and it's lost.

11   Choosing your words carefully isn't simply a recommendation. It's a responsibility.

12   A story is never completely your own.

13   Characters, like children, all have pieces of you in them, but your control over how they turn out is largely illusory.

14 Writers who cannot love their own
    characters are poor choices for companions.

15 Sometimes to make sense,
    you must make nonsense.

16 Make yourself a gift of irrational conversation.

17 Sometimes to find the light you have to peek
    into the dark.

18 Never ignore a child's questions.
    Never ignore anybody's questions.

19 Sometimes you have to ignore your story to
    tell it truthfully.

20 Sometimes a sentence drawn from a hat is
    better than one long considered.

21 When in doubt, turn things upside down.

22 When telling tales: demand a good price
    from strangers, but share generously with
    the child who asks for one more.

23 Sometimes to find a story you have to lose
    a few words.

24 If you don't know what else to say, write
    about not knowing what else to say.

25 Choose carefully the stories you tell,
    and, just as carefully, the ones you don't.
    Both will live inside your children after
    you're gone.

8

HITTING THE QUARTER-MARK

Fear shies away from being directly observed. So do electrons and alien cultures, truth and reality, and whatever we mean by "the divine."

Anticipatory by nature and definition, fear is an act of imagination, of pure creativity. We're afraid of things that haven't happened yet. Once they've happened—which is to say, taken form—it isn't fear anymore but grief or horror or despair or maybe relief. Writing and reading about fear—which is to say, giving it form—turns it into something else. Somewhere in the space between being afraid and giving it form, something important can happen.

Everything we're telling you here is true. That's the best we can do.

✶ ✶ ✹ ✶ ✶

Let's imagine they've been married now for fifty years.

They have come to resemble each other, as often happens to those in a profound relationship—husbands and wives, parents and children, owners and pets, prisoners and guards, teachers and students, gods and worshipers. The bones of their faces are wide, the flesh soft and softly wrinkled in patterns that go together. Their hands, separate or, most often, touching (though not often clasped anymore, because holding on too tightly hurts them both), are bent in many of the same ways, ring fingers similarly indented. Each of their bodies bears evidence of a lifetime of coming into contact with things, more like body art now than scars, and they more or less remember many of the stories behind the marks, though there's not much call for telling them again: kitchen injuries; the hammer poorly aimed on a high roof on a summer afternoon made hallucinatory by the fumes of hot tar; the gouging oarlock on an overturning canoe; the childhood fall down cellar steps; the car accident.

They're set in their ways, which are different from the ways in which they thought they were set a decade or five decades ago, different again from the ways still to come. Toast and grapefruit juice for breakfast, and for each a single mug of something, his mug the one with blue stripes and hers with teddy bears; on Saturdays, also a soft-boiled egg apiece. A walk at mid-morning and, most days, another after dinner. Every afternoon a phone call from their younger daughter, every Sunday a visit from the older, the occasional lunch with their younger son, calls from their older son usually from prison. The routines, even the ones that make them sad, calm the anxiety they each would otherwise have to handle in some other way, but do nothing to keep away Steve's fear.

Always part of his make-up, one of the countless things that attracted Melanie to him in the first place, Steve's fear has intensified over the years as he has become more and more himself. Sometimes Melanie thinks she can't stand it anymore. Sometimes his terror and his bravery in the face of it, the way he loves life anyway, endear him to her anew, arouse passion to new intensity. Sometimes, she's scared, too.

"What are you so scared of?" Melanie has fallen into the habit of asking him way too often. Hunched over in his chair, he can't answer because the gravity of his spirit has suddenly increased, implications and consequences have come down on him, and he cannot see himself upright under the weight. "What are you seeing that I'm not?" and he cannot bring himself to tell her, about the shadow that clouds his blood, that turns and tears cells from their moorings, that spins and grows until it cleans out all nerve, all tissue, all memory, filling every place he lives until there is no place left for living, darkening the sky and flooding the ground, bringing down his terror on anyone who might stray below.

Melanie has an inkling, though. They've been married almost fifty years, and Steve's fear has always been the other partner in their *ménage a trois.* When they were young and first in love and she'd begun to realize what a troubled child he'd been, she'd sometimes been afraid herself of trying to make a life with this man, and sometimes had wished with all her heart she could travel through time and space to tell him, "Sweet boy, don't be scared."

Her whisper, coming out of his blood and heartbeat and the air passing through his lungs and the stream of voices into and out of which everybody steps time and time again, would scare him, would provide further proof—as if any were needed—that there was plenty in this world and in the invisible world to be afraid of. He would dive back under the covers. She'd dive under there with him, determined to comfort him whether it was in his best interests or not.

"Don't be scared. You're safe. You'll be safe with me." That isn't exactly a lie. It's just not the whole truth, and he would know it. He would sing the ditty he'd made up to comfort himself, in the way that teenaged girls comfort themselves by cutting on their arms. Melanie can hardly bear to think of the child who is now her husband singing this little song, but he would sing it there under the covers to keep her at a distance he'd imagine to be safe. "Nobody loves me, nobody cares for me, I am all alone. . . ."

"You're not all alone."

"Am so!" He would be fierce, insisting on the view of the world he needs. "I am so alone." Singing again: "I am all alone. . . ."

"You won't always be," she would promise that little boy if she could. "Someday, when you're a grown man, you'll have a family who will love you more than you can imagine. More even than you'll be able to imagine then."

Maybe the frightened and lonely little boy would take comfort in that, if she could cross time and space to tell him. Just as likely, this message from beyond would terrify him and send him farther into himself.

In any case, she'd be doing it more for herself than for him. Because *she* couldn't bear to think of his pain. Because *she* didn't want him to have been so unhappy. Because she loves him more than anyone can imagine.

And Steve had turned out to be the sanest person she knew. If she had been able to change things for that little boy hiding under the covers in a room designated forever not his, if she could have sent him her message, she would have been getting in his way, interrupting. Steve hates being interrupted.

She couldn't always help it, though. Even after all their conversations over all the years, she couldn't always tell when he'd said what he wanted to say, and she'd start talking at the wrong time, and he'd snap, "Let me finish!"

She'd whisper over the years and the miles, "Don't be scared. Please don't be scared," thereby keeping him from singing the song it was in him to sing.

So now she tries to stay with, "What is it, Steve? What's making you so scared?" He can't tell her about the figure in the ceiling shadows staring at him with eyes that turn over a hundred times a minute, the dark holes at their centers taking him where he desperately does not want to go. She knows, though. There's a figure on the ceiling for her, too—not the same as Steve's, but close enough.

"Look," she says to him. "The bird's still there. But you wouldn't be able to tell it's a bird if you didn't already know."

He thought she hadn't seen the bird that had

caught its foot along the edge of the roof and dangled outside the kitchen window, dying in plain view and there was nothing he could do about it. He thought she'd been protected by her own way of seeing the world, or somehow he'd protected her and their girls and their little boy dead so many years. And their youngest son, the child they would not have had if Anthony hadn't died—how could that be? Now he sees, at the moment of Melanie's comment—which has the air of someone appreciating a sad and beautiful work of art—how ridiculous and how disrespectful it is to think any of them wouldn't or shouldn't notice.

The bird has been hanging there for the better part of a year. Wind made it seem to struggle; at first, it doubtless really did struggle. Decay made it shrink and twist. Before long, decay will make it disappear.

It's hard for Steve to tell if the man on the ceiling struggles, or if that's an illusion brought on by the movement of air. Sometimes the man on the ceiling grows thin when nobody notices him for a while, and then he'll be as fat as kidnapped babies, as bloated spiders in a web. He might hang there for years without moving, reduced to a ceiling stain or an inconsequential bit of decoration. But sooner or later he will come down.

"Look, Steve."

But Steve isn't about to look. He knows what he'll see. The man on the ceiling is gathering himself together to fill the sky. He is a flock. He is a multitude. He stretches his arms sideways like the wings of a bomber. He drops one by one from the ceiling until the roar of him drowns out all other sound. He multiplies daily, a little bit of death hiding in every gesture. He is the snarling dog at the end of the alley, the loose board in the stairs, the fever that will not break, the accident waiting to happen. He hangs there, waiting, ready to drop down when we least expect it, or when we most expect it, our expectations or lack thereof being of no consequence to him. He is the horror that rises from the underworld and descends from the heavens. He is the shadow that falls with each step through the world, the bitter taste after each breath. He is part and parcel.

Steve can get lost in the seductive poetry of being afraid. Melanie is determined not to let him, although she does despair. When she hears him mutter, probably not even to her, "Something is about to happen. Something is about to change," she loses patience.

"Oh, for heaven's sake!" she snaps at him. "Something is always about to happen. That's life, Steve. We're always on the cusp of change. Everything that happens to us changes our lives."

He doesn't hear it. He doesn't want to hear it. He knows she's right, everything changes, something is always about to happen, but he doesn't have to like it. Change, he has gotten into the habit of declaring, sucks. He's not always aware of it. He's not always this afraid. When he's not afraid, something might sneak up on him. Can't have that.

For a long time, the first intimation of disaster (and there were plenty) would send Steve out for a drive. Partly this was for the very reason that he fully expected to die in a car from a confluence of fate and inattention. The point was not to *get* anywhere, either geographically or with regard to whatever problem was preoccupying him. He just drove and worried, for their own sake.

One night in college he'd been driving and worrying about a girl. It was very dark, very late, very quiet. He wasn't getting anywhere. Suddenly the car pulsed with calamitous noise and brilliance, and he looked up to see the front-end of a locomotive filling the passenger window. He stomped the gas pedal and sped a block or so until he could catch his breath. Then he continued his driving ruminations, no more alert to real danger than before, having added the locomotive to his box of boogeybears, disasters, and spooks.

A couple of years later it was another woman who fueled his automotive meditations as he drove from town to town along Colorado's Front Range. He was falling in love, and it felt, among other things, like impending disaster. This time he let speed get away from him, and when he finally looked up it was a cement truck filling the windshield. A jerk of the steering wheel rocked the car off two wheels as he sailed into the next lane. At that precise time and place, the lane was clear. "Shit," he remarked aloud, and kept on driving, speed not much reduced, on his way to see the woman who would become his wife.

When they told him his son was dead, he got in his car and drove. The spring evening was clear, the interstate into the mountains nearly empty. He flew. He did not drive off a cliff, although there were invitations. Only much later did he realize that Melanie and their daughter had had to take a taxi home from the hospital. They never said anything to him about it.

We tell each other fearful stories. Not to banish or deny or even calm the fear, but to give it form, to call it out and make its acquaintance. Sharp edges wait for us in the darkness, attached to hands, which are in turn attached to murderers, rapists, dark hitchhikers, faceless beasts whose shambling is like a parody of our own cautious movements. We spend much of our lives avoiding shadowed places, bad neighborhoods, colorful cities and open spaces and depths and heights. For we know how sharp edges can tear, leaving scars that never perfectly heal. In our food, exotic insects have laid their eggs, tiny and protectively colored to blend in with our macaroni, peas, and fruit slices. Ingesting them sometimes makes us immediately and violently ill, our guts twisting and turning inside out. Worse is when the eggs lie dormant for decades, finally hatching when our stamina is at its lowest ebb. Someone has switched our baby, someone lives in our attic crawl space, someone has stolen our grandmother's corpse and now drinks tea and watches television with our grandmother dressed in clothing that would have embarrassed her. An alligator lives in our sewer line. A murderer waits for us in that shaded lane. In the sky beyond those mountains, aliens are gathering like flies around a corpse.

He has memories, but he thinks they might be memories of dreams, and he can't decide if that would make them more or less true. Catapulted from deep sleep by the unearthly howl of sirens that he was simply unable to believe could be mechanically generated, he imagined people kept out of sight there in his home town whose only purpose was to be periodically trotted out to give these warnings with mouths trained by years of insanity. The warning itself was unmistakable: a tornado was coming, and given the number of voices that had been gathered together, Steve knew it must be of great size. The ambient light had taken on a decidedly sinister yellow-gray patina. The air pressure had changed, and he had trouble breathing. The sky had thickened and darkened. Something was moving in. Something was about to happen. Something was about to change.

No matter what their initial form—tropical hurricane, Midwest-style tornado, tiny dust devil suddenly appearing at the end of the driveway—the storms would always grow and warp rapidly, turning sideways and filling the town in the valley below Steve's house: this great revolving wind, this mandala of torment, this depthless eye of some unknowable deity. Steve was afraid of God, who knew of all secret sins (of which there were many, including things Steve strongly suspected were sins but didn't know for sure—like seeing what couldn't be there, and imagining what was rude to imagine), which could easily be confused with Santa Claus knowing "if you've been bad or good so be good for goodness sake."

Again and again, he found a car with a key in the ignition or whose ignition would accept one of the keys in his pocket.

Again and again, as disaster loomed, he drove.

Once he'd discovered Yeats's "The Second Coming," he'd incant its lines from behind the wheel in an Orson Welles-like voice: *Turning and turning* and *falcon* and *true anarchy*. He thinks now that he barely comprehended the words, but they thrilled him and filled him with dread. *Things fall apart; the centre cannot hold.* More likely, the center would hold forever and suck him in.

The wind would intensify, or fall into an eerie calm. Sometimes it rained. Steve drove. At some point the circle of wind always turned like a hoop snake and tore the ground and the dead flew into the air. Steve drove, whispering and howling Yeats's or his own somber words. If he ever stopped, some other disaster would follow: fire, agitated by these winds, would sweep in from the west like a riot of red and orange spirits, malforming the trees and breaking the backs of the houses. Or water an oily blend of amber and blue would seep up out of the ground, dissolving all the familiar places as great, handlike waves reached up to yank him from behind the wheel.

He was terrified. He was also strangely excited, avidly wondering what might happen next.

Once, he remembers clearly, he did manage to stir himself to speed away from the pursuing wind: a dark, stinger-shape of a tornado, darting here and there on the landscape to pierce and explode whatever it touched. As fast as he could, much faster than he dared, he drove to a place where he had heard a shelter had been built into the side of a mountain, obscured by kudzu and dark itself, but safer than being out here on the open road. The tornado sewed the ground behind him with needles of splintered wood and a thread of braided earth. He stopped the car in the mud and was out and running before the engine had died, ripping apart the ravenous vines and on the first try finding the door to the shelter that really existed, desperately lowering himself into the dark and violent hole. Just as his head sank below ground level, the tornado struck, and all hell broke loose inches above him. Things fell on him, hurting, bruising, bouncing off. There wasn't enough air. But he was out of the storm.

Halfway down, though, he felt the shaft begin to contort around him, pinching his skin and yanking at his bones. The light around him turned red and wet. He realized that what he had mistaken for shelter was the heart of the tornado itself, its howl so loud it would fracture his skull because it wasn't the tornado after all, its howl so loud because what he had climbed down into was the throat of his father, whose rage and pain spun the world.

★ ★ ★ ★ ★

Steve doesn't like to drive anymore. He jokes that the one advantage of Alzheimer's would be that then Melanie and the kids wouldn't let him.

"Steve," says Melanie, "what's making you so afraid? There's nothing to be afraid of, honey. We're safe." He doesn't answer, which is probably just as well. Seeing that he's dozed off, she kisses his haggard cheek and goes to make dinner. Maybe she can get him to eat something tonight.

It's almost five o'clock; Katy's mother will be dropping her off soon. Melanie will make her special macaroni and cheese. Once Katy said to her, with that heart-stopping solemnity that has been characteristic of her since before she could talk, "Grandma, your macaroni and cheese is the best in the world." So Melanie makes it almost every time

Katy comes for a meal, and is afraid to ask if the child's taste might have changed. If there's a jar of applesauce in the cupboard, which she thinks there is, that would be nice with macaroni and cheese; Steve sometimes likes applesauce.

It isn't that Melanie is never afraid. Like most others of her species, she's probably encountered primal fear, as well as primal bliss and irritability and curiosity and hunger and satiation, from the moment of birth, maybe from the moment of conception. Maybe even earlier; she's not sure what she believes about that. She was about eight, Katy's age, the first time she was aware of being scared—really scared, scared to her bones, soul-scared.

As long as she could remember, her mother had been taking Melanie, in a rather desultory and uncommitted fashion, to either the little red Methodist church or the little white Lutheran church in the nearest town. Melanie never could detect much difference between the two, and she didn't think her mother could, either. Both had organ music and stained glass windows. From both, you came out of a dim sanctuary into bells and bright light—this having been northwest Pennsylvania, probably not sunshine as often as she now seems to recall.

The two churches never made much of an impact on her, beyond a vague sense of comfort that probably had more to do with music and light and cookies than with God. Not much about either of them would she as an adult term spiritual. But the religion was nothing if not organized.

Her father had spurned the Methodists and Lutherans; she'd picked up his scorn. Finally his proud agnosticism took the family to the Unitarians in the big columned brick building on the square—called Diamond Park, which encouraged the space to be regarded from its tip rather than its straight side—of the larger town eleven miles away.

Organized socially, politically, and intellectually rather than spiritually, but definitely organized, the Unitarians claimed to have no creed. But Melanie, perhaps out of her own need to tame the nature of the most important things by imposing human order, believed these wise, warm people, whom her revered father obviously revered, were teaching that there was no afterlife.

That heaven and hell were metaphors—which is to say, in the parlance of an eight-year-old, lies. That when you died you were just *dead*, you just didn't exist any more. And, in some way which made use of both instinct and developing cognition, she really, really understood.

What began then to visit her in the night was mortal fear pure and simple, direct, utterly un-metaphorical. No monsters under the bed. No white-gowned ladies raising knives. With the force of epiphany, she was suddenly terrified of death.

Crying herself to sleep replaced the gentle self-stimulation and release that had long been her bedtime ritual. Now, the moment she started slipping into unconsciousness, it would feel like dying and she'd scream herself awake. Or she'd leap out of sleep as if pursued by God or the Devil, heart in her ears. Hardly ever was she afraid of anything during the day, but at night fear of death, once discovered, wouldn't leave her alone.

When this started, her father or mother would come to her. She never doubted their love, but this might have been the first time she doubted their omnipotence. They didn't know what to do. They didn't know what to say. Later, amused, Melanie would realize they hadn't known what to do or say about the masturbation, either.

They'd sit with her for a while, and she'd calm herself enough to get them to leave because she didn't want to upset them and because their helplessness made the fear worse. Eventually they didn't come in anymore, and that seemed right. Even then, it was obvious to her that she had to do this alone.

The cuckoo clock in the living room strikes 5:00. It has run slow for as long as Steve can remember. He tries not to read anything into its persistent loss of time, only reminds himself of the fact—not really a fact, more a construct, a necessary but not fundamental imposed order—that the correct time is a few minutes after five. Though he's seldom hungry, he likes the sounds Melanie makes in the kitchen.

More and more frequently, thoughts enter his mind like beads on a string, discrete, in some way connected but willing to fly off at the slightest tug. He's learned to stay still for them:

We've brought it all upon ourselves, just by staying alive.

The terrors of the world are hungry by nature and they smell our independent brain.

The shadows in the dark are changing and soon will come after us one by one.

Melanie is singing. Steve thinks he might sing, too. By the clock on the kitchen radio it's 5:09; the microwave clock says 5:10. Melanie is thinking about the wilderness canoe trip she took a number of summers ago with Joe, who was then fifteen but still willing to spend ten days on a lake in the northern Canadian wilderness with his mother and six people he didn't know. She wonders if he'd be willing now, if he had the chance. She wonders if she would be.

It's 5:10, or 5:11, or, by the cuckoo clock, 5:07. Steve sits still for the thought to surface in his mind: it is essential that we learn how to live in a world full of monsters. When they put ashore and started setting up camp the second night out on the adventure she could not believe she'd signed up for, Melanie abruptly began trembling and her breath turned fast and shallow. Having expected to be frightened at the beginning of the trip and then been only excited and amazed to be doing this, she felt both ambushed and vindicated when the fear came now, hot and strong. On more than one adventure in her life she'd learned and then forgotten that fear has its own rhythms and will be met when it will be met.

She kept losing her footing in the mud. Three times she pounded the same tent stake in at different wrong angles, so of course it wouldn't hold. Her shoulders ached from eight hours at the oars. Need for a hot shower was urgent; anticipation of nine more days without one approached misery. She'd never set up a tent until last night. She'd never before been camping in her adult life. The only other time she'd been in a canoe was decades earlier at Camp Wa-Lu-Hi-Yi, and of that she remembered only the fact of it, no sensory detail or emotional residue, as if what she remembered was being told about it.

But physical discomfort and situational uncertainty were not what had her hyperventilating on the canvas floor of the tent, knees drawn up, arms crossed hard over her belly. This was mortal terror, and she had felt it before.

She's been told that when her visual disability was discovered, her parents withdrew in shock and grief and guilt, and the doctor recommended she be sent a hundred miles away to the School for the Blind. The infant Melanie must have sensed the abandonment and threatened abandonment, must have felt unloved and unworthy and alone, though it was not anyone's fault and though it took her parents only a little while to regain most of their equilibrium and proceed with raising a handicapped child. They did not send her away. But at her core, as at the core of the species, there is aloneness. Also at the core are community, connection, the myriad forms of love. And, perhaps at the core of the core, a borderless, impersonal sense of belonging, a transcendent sense of place that is most comforting and most terrifying of all.

She was afraid like that on her first silent weekend retreat. "Noble silence," they called it, for linguistic and theological reasons she hasn't yet figured out; not only did you not talk for two days, but you also didn't use gestures or body language, make eye contact, acknowledge another's presence or allow your own to be acknowledged. You were alone, in the nobly silent company of others who were alone. Why should that be terrifying? Why should it feel like death? She goes on silent weekend retreats as often as she can find them.

She'd been afraid at the house in the mountains by herself. It was the borderlessness that got to her, even within the borders of a short, pre-defined, self-initiated stay. Although the silence was by no means complete, its shape continually squished and stretched, amoebic, searching for a container. She could eat, sleep, write, take a bath any time she wanted to, and there was little reason to do any of those things at one time rather than another. When she climbed down the rough, steep slope to sit on a head-high boulder with her back against a lodgepole pine, she could hear airplanes, construction equipment, barking dogs, entire conversations not even in the distance, but those sounds had no more to do with her personally than did the susurrus of wind in pines, and nobody knew she was there except the worried spaniel who, too fat and bow-legged and cranky to clamber up beside her, glowered at her from the base of the rock. Disoriented and frightened, she went there often, and the spaniel, not entertaining the option of staying behind, never forgave her.

She'd been afraid like that again when suddenly her vision changed and she didn't know where she was in space and something *moved*.

Just at the horizon of her newly-truncated field of vision, something moved. Melanie didn't precisely see but somehow perceived all sorts of benign motion, none of which could account for this terror: Sunlight across a wooden floor. Shadows of leaves in a breeze. The curve of the chair rocker under her own weight. Inability to identify anything to fear intensified her fear. She could hardly breathe.

Something moved. Why should that be terrifying?

Mindful of her retina newly detached and partially, precariously repaired, she overrode the self-defensive instinct to snap her head around toward the danger. Instead, face approximately parallel to the floor per doctor's orders, she pivoted smoothly, stealthily, on the off-chance of catching the fear in the act. She knew she was opening herself to both discovery and disaster.

Sunlight, leaf-shadows, rocker motion, the black-and-white cat coming as usual to investigate human distress. Whatever the danger was, it was outside her field of vision, always had been and always would be.

Enormous wings. High black wind. Rustling and flapping loud enough to break the sound barrier, to break all barriers. She cried out, dodged, covered her head.

The very edge of a precipice under her feet, under her knees, under her chest when she flung herself sobbing to the floor. "I've never known you to be like this," Steve said, and she couldn't answer but thought wildly, *That's right. You haven't. Neither have I.*

And then at the eye of the rising, swirling purple and black, a flash of awe made itself known, awe rather than fear, the pearl in the dragon's mouth, the fire at the heart of the world.

All this because her vision had changed, and not even significantly; it wasn't as if she'd ever been fully sighted. All this because she no longer knew where she was in space and time. As if she ever really had. As if anybody does.

So here she was again, terrified in some way that felt primal and primordial, curled up in the tent that probably wouldn't stay upright through the night. The young guide came and settled herself—wisely, outside the tent, making her presence known through the mesh in the closed flap without approaching too near. "How you doin', Melanie?"

Melanie managed to breathe hello and thank you, but was caught up in a fierce, repetitive internal dialogue: "I can't do this!" "And what do you imagine you'll do instead?"

The thought rolls into Steve's mind like a loose bead: it is crucial that we name all the parts of the country where we live.

"I can't do this! I can't! I can't do this!"

In their introduction, the guides had announced—rather gleefully, Melanie thought—that this was, in fact, a wilderness trip, and in a real emergency the Royal Canadian Mounted Police would have to trek in to the rescue. Even Melanie, even in her escalating panic, didn't think this called for the Mounties. In part, she was embarrassed. The fact that she could identify nothing to be afraid of made her feel both foolish and more afraid. Anxiety about whether she had the physical stamina to keep up would have been understandable—the oldest in the group by at least twenty years, and not especially athletic, she had expected to feel a little out of place and wary. She had not expected terror, raising its knife. Adrenaline looped through her like a siren. She couldn't stop shaking. Maybe the organism recognized a threat the conscious mind could not. Maybe she really was in mortal danger, from a source unknown and unknowable. Maybe she always had been.

Twilight over Lake Nipigon unnerved her, and she couldn't imagine why. Everybody else, even Joe, was exclaiming over the beauty of sunset reflected in water reflected in sky reflected in water, and Melanie could tell that it was beautiful, but she found it spooky. Birds called. The surface of the lake was broken repeatedly by creatures who didn't show themselves. Large animal tracks cratered the sand. But she was not afraid of the birds, or the jumping fish, or whatever had made the tracks, even if, as her son hopefully suggested, it was a bear. She was afraid, somehow, of the light on the water, and being afraid of that was terrifying.

The guide spoke comfortably, as if they both had all the time in the world. "What you're feeling is pretty common. We call it hitting the quarter-mark."

Because Melanie didn't know the term, it sounded exotic, arcane. "Hitting what?"

"The quarter-mark. About a quarter of the way into the trip, a lot of people get panicky. Especially first-timers."

And do the Mounties come to the rescue?" She tried to laugh.

"You don't need rescuing. Just go with it and you'll be fine."

The guide's kindness and competence allowed her not so much to feel safe as to accept feeling profoundly unsafe. Now she dumps multi-colored pasta into boiling water, Melanie remembers, and her eyes fill with grateful tears. The fear ran its course. Before she came out of that particular wilderness, she would feel many other things: exhilaration, exhaustion, intense physical dis-comfort, intense physical satisfaction, uneasiness, peace, comradeship with her son, estrangement from him. She would not again, on that trip, know terror. Twilight on Lake Nipigon, a particular and not entirely visual opalescence, would stay with her for the rest of her life.

Steve is allowing space in his mind for two glittery spherical thoughts that carom off each other: There will always be intruders in our bedrooms, insisting they aren't intruders at all, they belong there as much as we do. And: There are angels and demons and giant goats and ladies in white, messengers who come from the eternal with important things to say.

It's 5:17 by at least one clock. Whisking flour into melted margarine and, while it's thickening in the microwave, grating the cheese—a task she finds tedious but can think of, with some bemusement, as a little self-sacrifice for someone she loves—Melanie is gazing dreamily out the west window over the sink at the quite different but also opalescent city twilight when a plane falls out of the sky.

Bored with his own ruminations, Steve is just getting up to help her set the table. He's not fast enough to avoid another bullet-like thought: These are our preparations, our practice sessions. These nightly assignations are our daily meals of darkness. He's both hungry and too full to take another bite.

Brief buzz of low-flying aircraft. A soft bang, like someone hitting a garbage can. Steve and Melanie turn to each other, as they've learned to do. "What—?" The power goes out. Yelling outside. Sirens, more sirens, mad and purposeful, terrifying in their intent to protect, all coming here.

Melanie has to tend to the cheese sauce, but Steve fumbles his way outside. The neighborhood reeks of airplane fuel. People are streaming onto the sidewalk and street and fire trucks are already pulling up. The neighbor kid insists a plane has gone down in the next block, but Steve knows better than to believe anything this loud and self-important boy says. When the cheese sauce can be left, though with unmelted lumps she won't be able to do anything about, Melanie finds flashlights, candles, and the little battery-operated television she and the kids have teased Steve for buying.

The story emerges. Two small planes, a Cessna and a Piper Cheyenne, have collided virtually over their house, which is the highest structure for several blocks around, a tall house and on a hill. One has landed upside down, with an eerie neatness between a neighbor's garage and the alley. Its sheared wing fell in another yard, a tire in another, a piece of the engine just off the street about a hundred yards from Melanie and Steve's back gate.

Early news reports say there's a body on the roof of the elementary school their kids went to. That turns out not to be true, and Steve and Melanie wonder to each other where that story came from.

The other plane went down into a house about seven blocks north, within sight of the bookstore, restaurants, newsstand, and candle shop Steve and Melanie frequent. The three people home at the time, including a fifteen-year-old on the phone when the plane crashed through his bedroom ceiling, and the neighbors and rescue workers who went in to do what they could, all got out just before the house exploded. Only minor injuries on the ground; nobody even hospitalized. All five people aboard the planes are dead.

The phone rings, rings again, callers on both lines. "My God, Mom, are you guys all right?" That's Veronica, needing details to help her relate to what's happened: How close was it to her old friend Wendy's house? Is there really a body on the roof of her old school? They acknowledge, though it's obvious, that Katy won't come over tonight; Melanie says to tell her they'll have macaroni and cheese another day, and hopes that's true. Steve gets on the phone to tell what he saw and heard.

Katy, who tends toward the dramatic, gets on the phone to ask if they're dead. Steve assures her they're not. Katy doesn't seem surprised that planes fell out of the sky. It's something any eight-year-old can understand. This is her hurricane, her tornado, her out-of-control fire and her rising flood.

Standing there with the receiver in his hand, ignoring the steady stream of calls coming in on the other line, trying to say what Katy needs him to say, Steve is suddenly enraged that this beloved little girl has to know that things fall out of the sky. "Look at children in the third world, the terrible things hanging over them," Melanie would say, thinking to make him feel better.

And of course it's true. Terrible things loom over the heads of most of the children of the world. Governments start wars and then send out for lunch. We're their waiters and waitresses trying to survive on their tips. Then we attempt to explain to our children why this has to be. We attempt to explain to our children who the bad guys are. We think if they believe our stories they'll be better for it. Fires bloom ever more spectacularly. Dark waters spread. The planes come down. The planes come down. Sometimes we forget how, in so many parts of the world, the planes come down on the heads of the children. And Steve hates it.

We don't want to hear about this because there is nothing we can do. Get a grip on yourself. It's just another evening in the world. The sun glows red. The breeze is sharp with jet fuel. Somewhere a cat trapped in a closet is clawing its way out. People make bad jokes about the neighborhood. In his grandbaby's eyes Steve can see the planes coming down.

How far can you go with this? How much can you handle? What do you imagine you'll do instead? You look beyond the planes and the metal, and you see dark angels falling out of the sky. You can see the man on the ceiling falling out of the sky. His arms are bent at strange angles. He makes motor farts with his lips and tongue, and despite her horror, Katy guffaws. You can see shadows stacked a hundred miles high falling out of the sky.

Steve tells himself to suck it up. This is the way life is; it's good for his granddaughter to find ways to cope. That might have been the most important task of being a father. Be reasonable, he chides himself as he tells Katy one more time that he loves her. Be a reasonable adult. But this is a child he loves beyond all reason. One of the many. He switches to the other line, and it's Joe calling to talk about the planes.

Melanie fixes tuna sandwiches and carrot sticks for their supper by flashlight. Usually they take the phone off the hook during meals so as not to be interrupted, a habit developed when they had teenagers in the house, but not tonight. Friends, co-workers, acquaintances leave messages when both lines are full. People from out of town, not quite sure of local geography, call to find out how close the crash was to them.

A Community TV reporter, trolling for witnesses not already snapped up by the commercial stations, insists they must have seen or heard *something*; Melanie finally hangs up on him, annoyed to have been suckered into giving him more time than she would ever give a telemarketer.

Everyone seems to have details to share, factual or not, and to want more. All this might be morbid curiosity or an ignoble desire to be part of the action, but it puts Steve in mind of how he sat in a chair the entire day after their son died while friends and neighbors came by downstairs to pay their respects. He thought he ought to go down and see those people but he couldn't climb out of that chair. Gravity had settled around him like cats, not to be disturbed. He was waiting. Waiting for certain colors to return, for his own voice to sound normal in his head. The world had taken a strange turn on its axis and he was waiting for it to make a small adjustment so he could live on it again.

That has never entirely come about. Not all the missing colors returned, and those that did have ever since had a slightly different quality. The voice he hears in his head when he speaks has never been the same. The world forever shows itself to be capable of strange, wild turns. Steve has had to make the adjustment on his own.

The chair he sat in all day after his son died is now in an attic studio where he draws and meditates. Covered by a throw, it's probably not recognizable to anybody else. It's the most comfortable chair in the house—gravity works differently in that chair. He thinks he'll go up there now. He takes a flashlight. It's no darker in the attic tonight than anywhere else, and there are no lights outside except from the flocks of helicopters buzzing very low overhead. Steve switches off the flashlight, sits in the comfortable chair, and waits.

Downstairs, Melanie is determined not to worry about Steve up there in the attic alone. The news reports are getting pretty thin, anchors straining to fill air time, reporters reaching for more to say when there is no more to say. The phone still rings continuously like a chain smoker lighting the next cigarette off the last. Melanie has had enough for tonight. Anyone who's heard about the crashes will also have heard that there were no serious injuries on the ground so should be able to extrapolate that she and Steve are okay. They'd be calling for some other reason, then—to make this thing real, to partake of it by proxy. She unplugs the phone.

She makes her way around the dark, quiet, cooling house, taking it all in. Every once in a while, reality puddles. She learned this many years ago from a young woman whose name is long since lost to her, about whom the only three things she remembers are that she had pale red hair and translucent skin, that she would not medicate her schizophrenia into submission because she valued the way it caused her to understand the world, and that one day she announced cheerfully to Melanie: "Reality flows and flows, and every once in a while, reality puddles." Melanie moves around her house, waiting for reality to puddle because planes have fallen out of the sky, right here and now.

Hours after Melanie and Steve have gone to bed—to stay warm, and because there's not much else to do—she to listen to a book on a battery-operated tape player, he to read old ghost stories by flashlight, a woman calls whom Melanie hasn't heard from in a decade, wanting to talk about the plane crash, wanting more to recount her divorce and remarriage and how she's started over. Half-asleep, Melanie asks her to call back the next day, but she never will and Melanie will wonder what that was all about.

The power comes on around midnight, hours earlier than had been predicted. Melanie stirs, sleepily proud of the cadre of public servants she doesn't very often think about. Steve gets up to shut off the lights, turn the furnace down to its night setting, reset the clocks.

Then he goes for a drive. He drives around the neighborhood. There's a moment when he looks up and an upside down airplane fills his windshield, but he knows it's not real.

The next morning he searches their property, including the roof, for plane debris and body parts. A reverse 911 call has given instructions about what to do if they find any. He doesn't. A police officer shows up in the afternoon for an official search. As will be widely reported the next week when the shuttle *Colombia* falls out of the sky over Texas, people carry off pieces as souvenirs. As if angels had died overhead, and now pieces of them were coming down with the breeze into lawns and gardens, backyard pools. Debris like ideas, like bits of memory.

Their granddaughter Christiana, Chris' daughter, comes over for lunch the next day. "Hi," she says, with studied nonchalance. "What are you doing?"

Stirring cheese sauce into macaroni, Melanie hugs her one-armed and answers the way Christiana would answer. "Nothin'. What are you doing?"

"Nothin'." Christiana stands there, hands at her sides, not looking at her grandmother.

Melanie turns her back and says with studied nonchalance she's learned from this very child, "So, did you hear about the plane crashes?"

Behind her there's an intake of breath. "Yeah! A block away from your house!" Christiana so seldom exclaims that Melanie chills.

After lunch, the three of them walk around the neighborhood. The police tape is gone. The streets are no longer cordoned off. The petroleum smell in the air is no stronger than if a spurt of rush hour traffic had just passed. When they join the other gawkers in the next block, there's nothing to see at the crash site except a metal storage shed tipped on its side and a dark stain on the ground that might have been made by spilled fuel. Melanie finds this eerie. "You'd never know anything happened here," she keeps saying.

Steve holds Christiana's hand, when she isn't too grown up for such a thing, and indulges in a fantasy about a shelter he could build to protect the people he loves beyond reason from things falling out of the sky. He gathers them together, his wife and children, grandchildren, other children he doesn't quite recognize, children and the shadows of children, children whose names are an incantation he cannot speak for fear that once he begins he'll never be able to stop.

He's stocked this room with everything they might ever need: food and water and medical supplies and drawing supplies and walls of books ("Good insulation if the power goes out," he tells everyone). Plastic and tapes and sheathing and filters to keep the invisible out, even though Steve knows full well there's nothing you can do to keep the invisible out.

And how strange it is because all his life he's counted on the invisible getting in. *But these are my children*, he thinks. *These are my children.* The little ones crawl across his back like cats, and he's amazed again at how small they are, or is it because of how large he's become? He really should do more about that, but at the moment he's pleased with the way his body spreads and holds them, and in fact feels too small for the enormity of the responsibility. The little ones laugh and call out each other's names, begging that one to watch this one's special trick, becoming suddenly so intent on the moment it frightens Steve, because that's when he's most aware of how real they've become in the world. Then one of them farts and their giggles wash across his body like bell song, and they point and point and giggle again until their grandmother shushes them and their parents shush them with promises of a story from Grandpa, a new old story they've never heard before.

But Steve can't think of what to say. So he sings a few lines he enjoyed when he was a boy, and then starts saying the words even though he doesn't have the words, he says the words, and they listen and even though he has no idea if they understand or even if they hear but at least they listen, as he says how it is to be here with them, as he says how it's been, as he says his testimony, of who he was and where he stood and what it was like to be here searching for the words.

After a while he notices Christiana singing. Not full out and with abandon the way Katy might sing, but almost under her breath, almost but not quite to herself. If nobody's interested, or if somebody's too interested, she'll contend she was singing to herself. Chanting, really, like a jump-rope song, most of its sense in the rhythm and not in the words. She skips to the rhythm of her words, glancing haughtily at the snarling dog at the end of an alley, and Melanie says to him, "Isn't she a miracle?"

He speaks over the breaking of his heart. "Yes."

"To think she wasn't in this world and now she is."

"And to think someday she won't be."

Melanie doesn't chide him or shush him or turn away from him. She takes his hand.

When Christiana notices her grandparents holding hands like the lovers they are, she'll tease them in the singsong way of young girls wondering about love and sex, scared and yearning and knowing she's helpless against it all. "Grandma's got a boyfriend! Grandma's got a boyfriend! Grandma and Poppy sittin' in a tree, k-i-s-s-i-n-g."

Christiana thinks boys are gross. Christiana loves to read and doesn't much like school. Christiana yearns for a puppy or a kitten, which she can't have in their apartment. Christiana's daddy has gone away because of a bad thing he did; she misses him, and it's a relief to have him gone, and she can't wait till she can see him again. Christiana is alive. Christiana will die.

Snow dusts the ground like flour. Then there are flakes the size of airplane debris, suddenly bleached and transcendent and beautiful. In the midst of this long drought, Steve is warmed by the snow and cold. "There's the engine," he points out to Melanie. "Part of the engine."

"Where?"

"There, in the mouth of the alley."

After a moment she says, "It could be anything. It just looks like a hunk of metal."

They're both thinking that it's only a few weeks until the anniversary of Anthony's death. Unlike most of their lives together, Melanie and Steve always do this thing apart. Of course it happened to both of them, but it would be perilous to forget that it happened to each of them as well.

Melanie will mark the day as she always has, by visiting the mountain where they were married and where they scattered his ashes or, if she can't get there, by walking in another quiet and beautiful place where she can find one pretty pebble to add to the collection Anthony had started. She sees a pretty stone now by the curb, thinks to pick it up, then decides it's not yet time.

Steve has never been back to the mountain. After his son died, Steve tried his best to imagine what it would be like when they saw each other again, what he would say, what Anthony would say to him. He made up story after story. He really wanted to believe them. But sometimes there's nothing to say.

For after years of storytelling, he realizes

there are places the words simply will not travel. Sometimes there's nothing you can say. You come up to the final truth of it, when it is so large you can't get around it, and it won't let you through, and you find you've run out of words, there are no words left to say. So you do the best you can. You make it up as you go along. You say *gah dedo longso may*. You say *whadie fego jungo defae. Mygee geeso reeso de nay. Whadada whadada u*. You can hear the planes falling out of the sky. You can hear the man on the ceiling howling on his final approach. You can hear the sky splitting open directly overhead. You call out your characters one by one and you grill them for answers. They speak back to you in tongues, and with all the voices of the living and the dead.

"Huh?" Christiana is beside him. "What'd you say, Poppy?"

He makes a face at her. *"Mygee geeso reeso de nay,"* he says in a funny voice. She giggles. He loves to make her laugh. "Silly Poppy," she says indulgently. He knows she knows this is not entirely play. He knows she doesn't entirely believe that planes really crashed and people really died. Is it his job to help her believe such a thing, or to protect her from that belief? Should he find her a souvenir she could take home and hide under her bed?

Steve rests his hand on his granddaughter's sturdy little back. Never varying her pace, she leans back into him, and her heart fills his hand, her pulse with his in his fingers, her life lines criss-crossing his. Her hair spreads over his wrist. Then she whoops and tickles him and runs off and runs back.

Later that evening, Christiana comes downstairs from the cheery grandkids' room where she so much wants to spend the night the way she used to but hasn't been able to for a while because something might happen to her mom if Christiana's not there. She stands close against her grandmother, hands at her sides, face hidden, silky black hair sweet against Melanie's lips. Knowing this child as well as she does, Melanie restrains her impulse to embrace her, another sacrifice for love.

"Honey, what's wrong?" No answer. "Are you scared?" The tiniest of nods against her belly. "Did you have a bad dream?" The tiniest of head shakes. "Can you tell me what's scaring you?" No answer. Resisting her characteristic impulse to keep asking, Melanie wonders if Christiana can hear her heart which right now she wills to beat only for this child. The rhythms of their breathing synchronize.

After a while Melanie offers cautiously, "You know what? When I was your age I was afraid of dying." A shuddering intake of breath. "Oh, sweetheart, that's it, isn't it?" No answer. Melanie's shirt is damp from Christiana's silent tears. They stand together in apprehension of the awful and awesome Mystery.

"Then when I was older I read a book by a man named James Agee called *A Death in the Family.*" Christiana is absolutely motionless. Maybe she won't understand what Melanie is about to tell her, but she loves reading and writing, and the quality of attentiveness between them is worth the try. "One of the things it's about is how the person who worries about death usually isn't the person who dies, because we change. We can't know how it will be for us until it happens. It made me less scared of death."

She doesn't say, though someday she will: It

was my introduction to the calm that can come from letting yourself float in the fundamentally unknowable without having to create sense and dimensions for it. She doesn't say: I've had to learn that over and over again, I'm learning it again right now, but not quite from scratch.

She does say, "That book made me want to be a writer."

Then, thinking of the little books the two of them have written and illustrated together since well before Christiana could read or write, Melanie suggests, "Would you like to write a book about it?" Long pause.

Then Christiana lifts her round wet face and regards her grandmother with a rare direct-ness that casts the moment in amber. "Not now, Grandma. Maybe later." Nodding, Melanie vows to hold her to it.

After dinner, after Christiana has again tried and not been able to stay the night, after Melanie has taken her home and they have watched the news together and she has gone to bed, comment-ing again on how you'd never know planes had fallen out of the sky just yesterday afternoon, Steve can't sleep. Disaster is imminent, and it doesn't help to assure himself that, if you look at it that way, disaster is always imminent, as is joy. He can't stand it. He puts on his cap, gets the car keys, lets himself out of the house and into the garage, and goes for a drive. He doesn't get anywhere. He gets lost for a while. When he rediscovers his own house in his own neighborhood, his own wife asleep inside not even aware that he's been gone, he slinks back inside and climbs the stairs to sit in the attic in the comfortable chair, shaking. No danger made itself known to him tonight, which intensifies his fear. The man on the ceiling is out there, on the ceiling of the world, masquerading as a star or a flock of night birds or the wingtip lights of a doomed plane, just waiting for the right moment to squash himself against Steve's windshield and make him drive off the road or into oncoming traffic, into the path of cars carrying everyone he's ever loved.

Moments cast in amber. Invisible rooms. Reality puddling. Breakthroughs from and into the divine. I hasten to protest: Steve and I don't *always* live like that! Not everything is fraught with Meaning. Like everybody else, we bumble through most of our daily lives attending to basic maintenance: doing laundry, going to the dentist, stocking up for whatever disaster might come, getting a haircut, walking the dogs, earning a living.

But even in the daily doing of what must be done, transcendence finds a way to creep in.

I'm a social worker for an adoption agency. Mostly I work with families adopting older kids who, because of abuse and neglect, have been taken away from their biological parents and need new ones. The job suits me, combining as it does a host of mundane details in service of a risky and world-changing endeavor. On my monthly required visit to an adoptive family, I sat at their dining room table and chatted with these extraordinary parents about healing. Their little boys, still toddlers, had increasingly been showing us that already they were on far more intimate terms with the man on the ceiling than any of us, in our naiveté, would have thought possible. My job is to be of help; I wasn't sure how much help I was being. The boys played under our feet.

Then the father said gently to me, "Well, you know, it's an asymptote."

"A what?"

He spelled it for me. "It's a mathematical term." He drew it for me on the back of one of the kids' drawings, a line on a graph coming closer and closer to the vertical axis and never quite reaching it.

"I probably learned that in geometry class, right?" But it seemed an utterly new term. My senses were hyper-alert. My skin was tingling. I knew this was one of those moments. The younger boy ran his Matchbox car across my shoe and giggled.

The father tapped his pencil on the paper. I noted that he had used a pencil, with a full eraser. "We can get closer and closer to helping them heal," he said, indicating the line that curved up and to the right. "And we've already come a long way from where we started," bouncing the tip of his pencil in the lower left quadrant where the curving line started. "But it's by nature an asymptote. We'll never get all the way there." He tapped the hypothetical point at which the line would cross the vertical axis.

The older boy said my name in his endearing way and offered me a plastic candy bar to pretend to eat. I did. He watched me closely to be sure I did it right. Trying my best, I said to his father, "Is that enough for you? Coming closer and closer? Because for some adoptive parents of traumatized children, it isn't, and once they realize they'll never get there, they give up."

The question seemed to surprise him. "Oh," he said, with what I took to be weariness and joy and great love in his voice, though I could have been wrong, since that's a lot to read into two words, "Sure."

I have his drawing on my wall, like the Little Prince's drawing of a sheep. Learning about asymptotes has changed my life.

But then, everything changes your life. Everything gets you closer and closer.

Our oldest son is in and out of our lives.

That's not precisely accurate. He's never fully out of our lives; he's our son. He's never fully in our lives, either; even on those very early mornings not so long ago when he and I sat together in the kitchen drinking coffee and talking about being a parent, being a child, being a sibling, being a life partner—talking, that is, about love, and how hard it is, and how necessary—even then, I never knew if we were really in touch.

By choice and by circumstance, the worlds Chris and I inhabit have only a few points of intersection. That there aren't more of them, and that they are so unreliable, is tragic. That there are any at all is a miracle. It's how you frame it at any given moment. It's a matter of which is foreground and which is background.

We first met our son on a winter day I remember as chilly, gray, windswept, at the farm where he and five or six other foster boys lived. He was ten. We had been married two months. None of us had any idea what we were doing. Not that, on those rare occasions when we are aware of being on the brink of a life-changing adventure, we ever know what we're doing; when it comes right down to it, every step every one of us takes is stepping out into the void.

Chris had been told who we were and what our intentions were toward him. He'd been waiting. On those long, straight, open high-plains roads. Our approach must have been visible for miles. The foster mother had managed to corral him into the house, but when he saw or heard us pull into the gravel driveway he hustled out the back door. We realized later that he must have seen us well before we saw him; at the time, we didn't feel his eyes on us.

He wouldn't come in. We sat in the living room of the farmhouse making small talk with the foster mother and the social worker, and every once in a while one of them would say, indicating the gray open space framed by windows on either end of the room, "There he is. There he goes again." We began to understand that our son was circling.

The foster mother was losing patience. A large, gray-haired woman without much noticeable warmth, she stomped in front of us to open the door and yell, "Chris! Get in here! You hear me? Get in here right now!" There was no response from our son; he certainly didn't obey her command. Scowling, the foster mother grumbled as she returned to her seat on the green couch that he never did as he was told. This would turn out to be a major understatement.

The social worker went outside. He was gone a while, and the foster mother excused but didn't explain herself and left the room, so Steve and I sat alone together in this stranger's house on the brink of becoming parents, waiting for our son to come to us. When the social worker returned he was flushed and breathless from the cold and the chase, and shaking his head in a sort of exhausted admiration for the defensive skill of this wounded, eager, cynical little boy.

The social worker—a bluff, stocky, blond man dispassionately accomplished at this work he'd been doing for many years—reported he'd used up his entire bag of tricks: light reassurance ("They won't bite you," a patently untrustworthy promise to a child who'd been bitten so many times in so many ways), grief work ("You're not going to live with your birth mom anymore. I know that's hard to hear. But you have to let her go"—advice nonsensical to Chris then and now), paradoxical intention ("You know what, Chris? You're not allowed to come inside. I don't want you to meet these people"—a game at which he'd more than met his match with this one).

Chris, the social worker told us, was running, strolling, kicking stones, climbing fences, chasing cats, following groundhog trails—doing all manner of things at the same time, but, under it all, circling. Getting closer, so that we'd see his pudgy form and sleek black hair and round face looking in the windows at us or pointedly not looking in. Swinging out as far as he could within the big fenced yard, maybe even going outside the fence at times although that wasn't allowed. Approaching us, but never quite getting there. Taking himself far away from us, but never quite all the way.

I don't remember how this standoff was resolved—the first of many; we're in one now. I'd like to report that Steve or I went outside and sat quietly somewhere on the unsheltered prairie until he could bring himself to come close. That's what we should have done. But we didn't know to do that. I'd like to tell you his need to attach won out over his need not to, finally and forever letting our son break free of the elastic line that had kept him spinning just out of reach, but that isn't what happened. I don't know what happened. I can't bring back to mind how we went from that point to the next and to this point where we are now.

Chris is well past thirty now, and still circling. So am I. I think we come very close to each other every once in a while, although I could be wrong. Then, I think, he shoots wildly out to the very farthest rim of the orbit. Either place is dangerous for all of us. Either place is, among many other things, love.

THE YELLOW CAT

Something Gabriella had noticed about cats was how they stared. They'd be sitting there all relaxed on the windowsill in the sun or on top of the laundry basket full of towels just out of the dryer or on her bed, and all of a sudden they'd be staring at something people couldn't see. You could tell by their eyes, or even if their back was to you and you didn't see their eyes.

She tried to stare like that. She tried to get really quiet and make her eyes go glassy and breathe in kind of a rhythm. But she never saw anything but what she always saw. Maybe that was because she was a person and not a cat. But maybe she could learn.

She liked thinking that people didn't see everything. She liked thinking that different people saw different stuff. Like Grandpa. He stared, too, and she thought he saw and heard and maybe smelled weird stuff. She liked that. It also gave her the creeps.

Gabriella's cat Cinnabar stared. Cinnabar was the name for some Chinese stone that was kind of a gold-red color, like her. She was an old cat, almost thirteen. Gabriella was thirteen, too, but it didn't mean the same thing in cat years. Cinnabar still played with yarn once in a while and she still rolled in the weeds and got her fur all clumpy and then wouldn't let you cut out the mats. Her favorite things were sleeping on Gabriella's head, eating tuna fish, and staring.

In Gabriella's opinion, "Cinnabar" was a weird name for a cat, but she didn't have anything to say about it because she wasn't even born yet when Cinnabar was born. That was a weird thing to think about. Where was she when Cinnabar was born? Where was Cinnabar before Cinnabar was born? Just lately she'd started to think about stuff like where did you come from and where did you go when you died? Mom said we'll never know, which made Gabriella mad. Not knowing stuff was dangerous.

Gabriella's grandpa never used to like cats.

Ever since he and Grandma came to live with Gabriella and her parents, he complained about Cinnabar's long yellow fur all over the place and how she clawed the furniture, and he'd say mean things like, "Cats don't care about anything but themselves," and "Cats are sneaky. You can't trust 'em as far as you can throw 'em." Gabriella used to be afraid he was going to throw Cinnabar or something, but as far as she knew he never did. He better not have.

She wasn't their real granddaughter. She was Dad and Mom's real daughter, because real wasn't about whether you were adopted or not. It was about something else, something about imagination. She didn't exactly understand it and she didn't want to think about it enough to figure it out.

She thought about it a lot anyway, in the back of her mind, kind of like the watercolor washes they had to do in art class, where you covered the whole paper with some pastel color and then painted stuff on top of it. What was real? What made Mom her real mom and Dad her real dad and herself their real daughter, when she wasn't born to them and most people, like most of her friends, thought that made it not real?

It had something to do with if you could imagine it. Mom and Dad could imagine it. She could imagine it, too. Grandpa and Grandma couldn't, or didn't want to. It was like their imagination muscle wasn't strong enough, or they were afraid for some reason. In a way, Gabriella understood that. Imagining yourself real *was* scary.

They were nice to her, usually, the way you'd be nice to somebody else's kid. It was like her being their granddaughter was this idea in this other world they couldn't quite get to, and so she couldn't quite get to it, either. Almost, but not quite. Closer and closer, but never all the way.

The ancient Egyptians thought cats could guide you through the underworld. That's why the Pharaohs buried cats with them in the pyramids, because they thought they'd need them in the underworld, which is where they thought you went when you died. Grandpa had told her that one time when she was little, and it had scared her, and she kept thinking about it, and finally she'd decided not to believe it. He didn't remember saying it, but she couldn't forget it. Now it was in her history book, too, and there was a big test on Monday, and she really couldn't stop thinking about it.

So she was sort of worried that it was the underworld Grandpa had one foot in and he'd try to take Cinnabar with him. She was worried that he'd go away and Cinnabar would go away and she'd never know what this underworld place was. She was even more worried that they'd try to take her with them, and that she would want to go.

Now she didn't think Grandpa even knew what a cat was. He was really old, and he had some kind of brain disease. He hummed more than he talked, not any actual song but just this noise like somebody twanging a rubber band. Most of the time he didn't know anybody, even Mom and she was his real daughter. That made Mom feel bad. Grandma was mad all the time. Mom said that was because she was scared, and besides, his humming drove her crazy. It was the first time Gabriella had thought about how being scared could make you mad.

Sometimes Gabriella wondered if Grandpa even knew who he was. Not just if he knew his own name, but if he knew who he was.

Sometimes Grandpa would get upset and he'd yell or make this kind of groan. Sometimes he looked all relaxed and peaceful. Gabriella would sit with him and hold his hand, or not touch him but just sit there and stare at him, and try to imagine what he was seeing.

It would be cool if she could see things like Cinnabar did or like Grandpa did or like anybody but a thirteen-year-old girl named Gabriella did. It would be scary, but it would be very cool.

Once in a while he talked to her. She didn't think he knew he was talking to her, exactly, but he said stuff that was weird and neat and creepy and nice. He said, "I love you" a lot, and he never used to. Mom told her he hardly ever said he loved her, either, even when she was little, which was really sad and made Mom's eyes fill with tears and made Gabriella wonder if maybe Mom wasn't his real daughter after all. She said she didn't think he knew how. Now he did.

One time he told Gabriella, "I've got a foot in

the other world already." He didn't explain what that other world was, but she sort of understood, and so she thought maybe it was that other world that he stared at.

One time he told her, or she just happened to be in earshot when he said, "There's a car waiting in the woods for me." She wanted to go there with him. She didn't ever want to go there. What she wanted was to know what it was like without ever quite having to go there herself.

Cinnabar sat on Grandpa's lap a lot. He petted her. Gabriella wasn't sure either one of them really knew the other one was there. Or maybe they both knew they were both there but it didn't matter who either one of them was. Whatever. She could get really confused thinking about that, and sometimes she couldn't stand to be around them because they made her feel too weird and left out.

But then she'd just sit in the same room with them, when Cinnabar was purring and Grandpa was humming and they were both staring. She'd quit trying to figure things out. She'd just sit there. Then sometimes she'd feel peaceful and excited at the same time, and sometimes she'd know the world was about to end.

Mom worried, but she worried about the wrong stuff. Parents did that a lot. "Gabriella." she'd say, "I'm sorry. I know it's hard having Grandpa and Grandma living with us."

It wasn't hard. It was weird, kind of, but it wasn't hard. Not any harder and not any weirder than having Cinnabar live with them, and she had been there longer than Gabriella had, so actually you'd have to say Gabriella was living with Cinnabar instead of the other way around and maybe that was weird and hard for Cinnabar.

Today was Saturday. It had snowed in the night and it was still snowing in the morning. When Gabriella got up, Cinnabar was on the windowsill of the bay window in the dining room, all straight and tall like those cats carved out of smooth wood, with just the tip of her tail twitching. Her feet made sort of a point and her shoulders were hunched up, so she was sort of shaped like a heart. Mom and Dad had a picture Gabriella had made when she was a little kid of a cat shaped like a heart and with feathers on its feet. It was dumb. She wished they wouldn't keep stuff like that, like it was important or something. She wished she'd just kept the heart-shaped cat with feathers a secret. Too late now. Whatever.

Cinnabar was probably watching the snow. Or maybe there was a bird or a squirrel in the vine. Sometimes in the spring the birds and squirrels would get surprised by a snowstorm and they'd get in between the vine and the window to keep warm, and you could see them right up close, like they didn't know you were there, or they knew you couldn't catch them through the glass, or they didn't know what you were. Gabriella wondered if there was a window she didn't know about and somebody or something was on the other side of it watching her, and if they could get to her they'd hurt her or they'd keep her safe, but they couldn't quite get to her.

"Gabby, go call Grandma and Grandpa for lunch," Mom said.

She was watching this funny movie, and she was all wrapped up in the blanket Grandma had made a long time ago out of these bright little squares called Granny squares, and she didn't want to get up. So she didn't.

"Gabriella."

"Okay." But she could wait. Mom wasn't yelling yet.

"Gabriella!"

"Okay! Whatever!" It wasn't fair. Why couldn't Mom go get Grandma and Grandpa herself? They were her parents. Gabriella got up, kept the afghan around her shoulders, stood in the doorway for a few more minutes to watch while the guy in the movie got a bucket of water dumped on his head, and then she went. She wasn't happy about it, but she went.

Cinnabar was still sitting on the windowsill, in the same spot, at the same angle. The tip of her tail was still twitching, exactly the same length of it, exactly the same distance back and forth, exactly the same speed. When Gabriella passed by her on the way to the back of the house where Dad had turned a couple of rooms into a little apartment for Grandma and Grandpa, she stood on tiptoe and looked down over Cinnabar's head.

Big surprise: she was staring. Her eyes were the same color as her fur and right now they were huge, and her ears pointed straight up. When

Gabriella moved back and forth, the cat's eyes didn't follow her.

She'd never seen Cinnabar stare *up* before. All the way to Grandpa and Grandma's, she wondered what was up there, and she wanted to see it, and she didn't want to.

Grandma said, "I can't go to lunch. He's having a bad day." She kind of smiled and winked, like the two of them had a secret together and Grandpa was left out of it.

"What's wrong?" This room that used to be the guest room and was now their living room, but Grandpa wasn't sitting in his favorite chair. Lately he hadn't always wanted to sit here, and Grandma and Mom were worried he'd get lost. Maybe he'd go to that other world. Maybe Gabriella could go with him. Just for a visit.

Grandma started to say, "He doesn't—" and then you could tell she decided Gabriella was just a kid. This time her smile was totally fake. "He's just a little confused, Gabby. You better go get your mother."

Gabriella got stubborn when adults thought they had secrets from her and she knew perfectly well what the secrets were. Maybe it was mean, but she asked, "What's the matter, doesn't he know you today, Grandma?" Usually she wouldn't ask something right out like that.

Grandma got tears in her eyes, and Gabriella felt terrible. For some reason, it had never occurred to her that somebody as old as Grandma would cry. That was one reason she didn't ask stuff right out: she was always afraid something important hadn't occurred to her.

Grandma sighed and went over to the stove to stir something in a pot. Gabriella smelled chicken noodle soup. Homemade. Campbell's was better. "Go get your mother. Please."

"You go. I'll stay with him." Why was she saying that? She didn't want to stay with him.

"You can't handle him. What would you do if he walked out of the house?"

Gabriella shrugged and made her voice sound like this was a dumb question, which it wasn't. "Whatever. Walk with him." It was the only thing she could come up with. She didn't know if it was right or not.

"He won't talk, you know. He just hums."

"I could hum with him."

Grandma glared at her, and Gabriella thought she ought to say that wasn't supposed to be a smart remark.

"What would you do if he called you by some other name? Say, Melanie?" Melanie was Mom's name.

"I wouldn't care." She would care. She was making this up.

Grandma sighed again. Finally she turned off the burner and put the lid back on the pot and said, "He's in bed. He won't get up. Maybe it would be okay for a few minutes. You can have some soup."

She was proud that Grandma would trust her. All of a sudden she was also scared to death. She actually didn't have a clue what she'd do if he started acting really really weird. She was going to do this wrong, whatever it was. She was always doing things wrong. She could think of a million ways she could mess this up.

For just a minute, she thought she might just not do anything. Stay here in the kitchen that used to be the family room and not eat any homemade chicken noodle soup and not take any to Grandpa, either. Grandma didn't *tell* her to give him soup. Or leave Grandpa alone and go hide in her room and say she thought Grandma was coming right back. Or run away.

Finally what she did was ladle some soup into two bowls, put spoons in them, and carry them into the other room, which used to be Mom's office and now was Grandma and Grandpa's bedroom. Cinnabar led the way, her tail up straight. Well, she didn't exactly lead, because you could tell she couldn't care less if Gabriella followed her or not. It was more like she showed the way. Guided. Gabriella hadn't noticed her come in, but she was glad for her company. If you could call it company. Maybe Cinnabar could show her what to do. Somebody better show her what to do.

Grandpa was propped up against a reading pillow. He was humming, and his one finger on top of the blue blanket was twitching like Cinnabar's tail. He didn't have his false teeth in so his mouth was all pushed in and disgusting, and he was staring up at the ceiling. Gabriella looked up there, too, but she didn't expect to see anything and she didn't.

"Grandpa." Her voice was a lot louder than she'd thought it was going to be, so she got embarrassed. "It's me, Gabby. Are you hungry? Grandma made us some chicken noodle soup."

He didn't pay any attention. Cinnabar jumped up on the bed and settled herself in front of him, where his lap would be if he had a lap, but his legs were too skinny and crooked to call it a lap anymore. She turned around with her back to him and sat up tall like a carved cat and the tip of her tail started twitching again.

"Okay, whatever." Gabriella gave up on the soup. Maybe Grandma would be mad, but Grandpa wasn't interested and she wasn't, either. She put the bowls on the dresser and then just stood there, trying to figure out what she was supposed to do.

If you didn't do what people wanted you to do, you got hurt. Even if you did, you got hurt. And they didn't tell you what they wanted you to do, or they changed their minds, or they tried to trick you. Grandpa wasn't telling. Cinnabar wasn't telling. Gabriella didn't know what to do. She was going to get hurt.

She took a couple of shaky steps toward the bed. Now she was looking down on them. Grandpa had been bald all her life. In fact, Mom had pictures of him when he was about twenty-five, and he was bald then. Right now the top of his bald head was shiny, and there were spots on it. The top of Cinnabar's head was furry, and a weed was stuck behind her ear, but Gabriella knew better than to try to get it out because Cinnabar would scratch.

She put her hand on the top of her own head. Her hair was all flat. She was sick of messing with it. She just wasn't good with hair.

Both of their eyes were turned upward. All four of their eyes, Cinnabar's golden and Grandpa's brown and just as glassy as the cat's. They were staring at something but definitely not at Gabriella.

Out loud she said, "Let me see." Just saying it out loud was scary. She didn't like calling attention to herself. Nobody answered. Nobody was ever going to answer. Mom and Dad promised they'd answer her, promised they'd be with her and go ahead of her and show her the way, but they weren't here right now, were they?

Then Cinnabar said—her name. It wasn't "Gabriella," but it was her name.

Grandpa said, "Come on. You can come with me. I'll show you." Or something like that. He got up. He almost fell, and Gabriella reached out and took his hand. She had to go with him or he'd fall or he'd get lost.

The three of them were moving. It wasn't walking or running or swimming or flying or any other word Gabriella could think of for ways you could move, but it was moving. Cinnabar went first, her tail straight up. She wasn't looking back, but Gabriella could tell they were supposed to follow her.

If she followed Cinnabar and Grandpa and went wherever it was they were going, she would get in trouble. If she didn't follow them, she would get in trouble. When Gabriella really thought about it, she knew she didn't get in trouble with Mom and Dad a lot, and she knew they wouldn't hurt her or leave her or quit loving her, no matter what she did, but down deeper she always knew it would happen, it would happen, down deep she was just a tiny baby and the big people who were supposed to take care of her got mad because she did something wrong, she was just a tiny baby and she did something wrong, and they grabbed her and yelled at her and then she was flying through the air and then her head hit the wall and broke. Her head broke. She did something wrong and she got in trouble and they broke her head.

She held onto Grandpa's hand. He didn't hold her hand back, but he didn't pull his hand away, either. She had to go with him or he'd get lost or she'd get lost.

They weren't going up or down, exactly, but more like *out* or maybe *in*, which somehow would feel the same. Or maybe the world, whatever world this was, was moving around them and they were standing still. When she tried to think about it that way she got kind of dizzy, like when she tried to think about the earth turning in space or the sun staying still and the earth rolling around it. The sun didn't actually rise or set, so why did people say "sunrise" and "sunset"? It was a trick.

Apparently they were outside now. She didn't recognize any of it, but Grandpa and Cinnabar seemed to. There were things like clouds that weren't clouds. There were things like angels and ghosts. There was something on the ceiling or the sky—except that it wasn't a ceiling or a sky—that kind of made her think of a huge spider, and she didn't like spiders, but it also made her think of a man, the shadow of a man, a paper-doll man come to hurt her and to guide her and to tell her secrets all at the same time, and to steal her away.

Cinnabar had feathers on her feet, and then she didn't. Grandpa was holding something out in front of her that Gabriella knew was a dragon's wing without the dragon. What would Grandpa do with a dragon's wing? What would she do if he gave it to her? Go look for the dragon?

What was a dragon anyway? Dragons didn't really exist, but she thought she knew what they were. She wouldn't say that to anybody but Cinnabar and Grandpa, and she wouldn't actually *say* it to them, but she knew what a dragon was. She'd met dragons before. She'd lived with a couple. She'd been born to them. Did that make her a dragon, too? What would it mean to be a dragon? Or a dragon's wing? If she kept thinking like that she was going to get lost.

So they walked—or swam or flew or rolled like the earth or slithered or whatever it was they were doing—for a long time. Or a millisecond. Or else it didn't have anything to do with time at all. Whatever.

They came to a big hump, or the hump pushed up in front of them. It reminded Gabriella of the snake-that-swallowed-an-elephant in *The Little Prince*. Maybe it was just a pile of leaves and branches, but she had the impression there was something hard inside like the armatures they used in art class when they were doing clay.

Grandpa hummed, "There it is. Waiting for me." Cinnabar must have buried herself in the hump of leaves. The leaves were almost the same color as she was, only duller, and they wriggled and poked up and jumped because the cat was moving around under there. Maybe it was the cat. Gabriella guessed it could be something else. She didn't know what.

Grandpa fell. Gabriella yelled, "Grandpa!" and grabbed his arm and tried to get him up. His arm was like a really thin branch and she thought maybe it would break and she'd be standing there holding half his arm like a broom. That would be embarrassing.

He jerked his arm away from her. He was a lot stronger than she'd thought. He fell again, but this time she realized that he didn't fall, he dived. Was that her fault because she didn't hold onto him? How could she hold onto him? And, anyway, he didn't want her to. No matter what she did, she was going to get in trouble.

When he threw himself onto the mound, he thumped, so it must be hard underneath just like she'd thought. She was sort of proud of herself that she'd known that. He was clawing with his hands to clear away the leaves and branches. Where was Cinnabar?

It was a car. There was the top of it, shiny and reddish-purple. There was a window, but you couldn't see inside. There was a door. Grandpa was working to get it open. She didn't know if she was supposed to help him or not. An old-fashioned car, funky, all rounded like a Beetle but squarer.

Grandpa got the door open. She didn't think it should have been that easy, but he was inside the car now, and Cinnabar was curled up on the dashboard like one of those fuzzy toys you hang from the rearview mirror, only bigger. Gabriella's eyes and nose itched from all the leaves, and her shoes were damp. How was she ever going to get Grandpa out of the car? She couldn't leave him here while she went to get help, so it was up to her.

"Grandpa, come on, let's go home." She jumped when the horn honked long and loud. She didn't like getting scared like that, and now she was mad. "Stop it!" she yelled, and the horn honked again. Fine, let him sit in there all he wanted, turning the steering wheel and stomping on the pedals and honking the horn. The car had been in the woods buried under leaves and dirt for a long time. It was amazing the horn worked. Obviously the engine wasn't going to start. Obviously Grandpa wasn't going to really drive, no matter what he thought because he was crazy and didn't know what was real and what was made up. He wasn't going anywhere.

The engine sputtered a few times and then started. The car moved, backed up. Big clouds of leaves and dust poofed, and she sneezed three times like she always sneezed. Grandpa was grinning at her through the cracks and bird doo-doo on the windshield. She'd never seen him grin like that before. Cinnabar was yellow like a fat pile of leaves on the dashboard. Grandpa honked the horn again and made that motion with his curled-up fingers that meant "come here."

She couldn't just let him drive off by himself. She couldn't let him and Cinnabar leave her. "Wait!" She started running after the car, which was moving pretty fast now, backward and downhill. She chased it and chased it, and her chest hurt and she was dizzy and her legs hurt and she got close, touched the headlight once and burned her fingertips. Old-car exhaust made her cough and choke. She got close enough to see that Grandpa had his eyes closed and his head down and he wasn't looking where he was going and he wasn't looking at her anymore.

But Cinnabar was. Cinnabar was sitting on the hood of the car, outside now, tall and straight like an Egyptian guide cat, and her yellow eyes were staring right at Gabriella like lights. When Gabriella pushed herself forward and got a hand on the door handle, Cinnabar hissed and jumped onto her face—flew, really, except cats can't fly.

Now Gabriella couldn't see. Her nose and mouth were full of Cinnabar's fur. All she could hear was hissing and purring, like Cinnabar was mad at her and loved her at the same time. She felt softness, and warmth, and Cinnabar's weight—less than you'd think because most of her was fur—and then she felt, for the second time in their lives together, two sharp pokes, one on each side of her head, Cinnabar's claws puncturing the skin at her temples.

"No," the cat told her. "Stop."

Gabriella burst into tears. Cinnabar pulled her claws out and dropped to the ground, landing on all four feet the way cats do. Gabriella touched her temples, afraid of what she'd find, but there wasn't any blood and now there wasn't any pain, just the memory of the cat's sharp claws. Cinnabar was gone. The car was gone. Grandpa was gone. She was all alone. She'd come close to something, but couldn't quite get there. She knew her way home.

Now Mom worries that being with Grandpa

and Cinnabar when they both died will scar Gabriella for life. Parents worry about all the wrong things.

Something is about to happen. The organism reacts to danger it cannot possibly identify, only the sense of danger, only the certainty. It curls up. It puffs itself up. It does everything in its power to make itself either ferocious or beneath notice, impermeable or absorbent, battling to keep the danger out or to take it in. It insists that naming will make the danger real and therefore manageable; it ought to know better by now. It comes as close as it can to the danger without actually encountering it.

Maybe the date on the big kitchen calendar has sounded the alarm, not starred like birthdays and adoption days and wedding anniversaries, instead circled or underlined, as if it could ever be forgotten. But children far too young to grasp the concept of a calendar seem to feel it, too, this sense of impending doom which is not impending at all but has already come to pass. Maybe it's the slant of light or the alteration of birdsong. But blind and deaf people feel it, too. Something, something dreadful, is about to happen, about to happen again.

Maybe it's the quality of the air, this year soft and smooth and carrying a fragrance that has nothing to do with flowers. But some years it's been wintry, and once or twice an early heat wave has implied that spring could be skipped altogether, and no matter what the weather, no matter how the air feels on its exposed surface, the organism knows that something, something is about to happen.

Maybe it's the state of the world; this year, like every other year in the history of the planet, there is much to dread. But this is the first March in fifteen years that war has been on this particular horizon; the others here have been awash with peace and plenty, though of course somewhere, for someone, they were not.

The dreadful thing has already happened, fifteen years ago next week, on a spring evening like this and not at all like this. Dread skulks and haunts, for no good reason. Fear is a fiery ghost of its former paler self, no body, only soul; until this thing happened, the forms fear knew to take were metaphorical, mythological.

Maybe it's the way the earth turns and tilts at this time of year, magnetic field shifting, molten core sloshing against strata that have been burned so many times before and seeping into hidden places to burn for the first time, though it has seemed for fifteen years that nothing could be hidden from this. Maybe it's the primal instinct to come up to the thing again and again, to come close and stare it in the face, to make its acquaintance. Knowing all the time, of course, that it can never quite be gotten at, it can never fully be claimed, it will always be just outside our reach.

* * ✯ * *

She was tiny and old and a nun. "What shall we talk about, Melanie?" she invited me once we were settled.

She must have been close to ninety when I first went to see her, and she'd been a nun since she was nineteen—she told me she'd wanted to join the convent right out of high school but her mother had insisted she wait a year, experience a little life first. I think she had herself a boyfriend during that year; she never quite said so, but there was a certain sparkle in her voice.

She was internationally known for her social and political activism, for her work on behalf of peace and civil rights, the ordination of women, and, of all things, abortion rights. She'd been one of the handful of American women invited by Pope John XXIII to be part of Vatican II. She was much revered, and utterly accessible.

"I want to learn how to live a contemplative life without being a hermit on a mountain top," I told her.

"Oh, but I'm not a contemplative. And I've never in my life been a hermit!" Her laugh was infectious.

"You've combined a spiritual life with an engaged life," I persisted, then took a breath before adding, "You're wise."

She accepted it as I'd meant it, neither a compliment nor a criticism, rather as if I'd observed that she was old. "You're wise, too," she said, and having just learned from her, I inclined my head and didn't rush to thank her or demur.

Probably she was more comfortable with the ensuing few minutes of silence than I was, but maybe her mind was just wandering; within the year the small strokes she'd already begun to experience would cause her to stop seeing students like me. A bird chirped like a metronome outside her window. The buzz of the lawnmower next door rose and fell and rose again. Two of the other nuns who shared the house started singing "She'll Be Comin' 'Round the Mountain" in the kitchen on the other side of the wall from where we sat.

She looked up and straight at me. "Suppose we get right down to it and talk about—do you mind if I use the word 'God'?"

"No—uh, no, not at all," I managed.

She nodded briskly. "It's as good a name as any, I guess."

This woman had been a Bride of Christ for seventy years. "Right," I said, "I guess." She was on her feet now, moving around the cozy little room. Watching her, I realized we were meeting in her bedroom. The bed was covered with a Winnie the Pooh quilt. At first I thought she was searching for something as she picked things up and put them down, but it quickly became evident that she was just looking, feeling, maybe smelling.

"The thing about God," she remarked cheerfully, "is that He's a Mystery. And that's just the way I like Him."

10
DOWN THE DARK STAIRS

Melanie has been teaching me lately about the asymptote, which is a way of talking about that goal you cannot achieve no matter how far you extend yourself, that state you cannot reach, that idea you cannot understand, that person who will not care for you the way you want them to care.

This is the way some of us live all of the time, and all of us live some of the time.

Melanie likes the mystery. It pleases her to know there are things beyond human ken and will. I often find it more frustrating than uplifting, but at the same time I'm not sure I'd have it any other way.

Understanding has always been the line I've worked toward, and for a while there I thought I was getting pretty close. Now I suspect I've been in a great orbit, coming close to at least a kind of understanding for so long, and now on the other side of the curve, leaving that particular line behind at the velocity of escape. I think I'm going to be okay with this.

Melanie and I are very different people in many ways. Her interests in jazz, long walks, bike-riding, and spirituality contrast notice-ably with my love of comics, movies, puppetry, cartoons, and trash TV. She is renewed through quiet and meditation, goes off on silent weekend retreats—*voluntarily*, mind you. People often assume I must enjoy that sort of thing as well, because I'm sometimes so quiet, so shy, so prone to listening without speaking, to the point that it makes others uncomfortable. That silence *is* necessary for me; I spend much of my life there. But it's not something I would ever say I enjoy. It is the medicine you hate the taste of but must have. I could not last more than an hour in a silent retreat. I could not spend that much time alone. I have been in that dark and quiet place, I have spent years in that dark and quiet place, and I know that someday it will be to that dark and quiet place I will return.

Our differences are the most interesting part

of our relationship to me, as are the differences between me and my children, and their differences from each other. Yet I can't say I'm immune to the anxiety many people feel when they realize how different they are from those they love: if we're so different, what holds us together? How close can we get, or how far, before simple physics spins us off in our own separate ways, the life we once had together forever out of our grasp?

What do we do with our time, how do we spend our time, to stave off the eventual darkness?

Do we meditate, do we write, do we make love, do we spend all day listening to music or watching cartoons?

How close can we get to making it all meaning-ful before it all seems meaningless again?

There are necessary angels down here, thou-sands of them. Sometimes the sound of their wings is no louder than eye blinks, but sometimes it's as thunderous as the crashing of planes.

There is a child down here who will not tell me his name. There is a palsied light in the huge eyes of creatures who shake without moving. There are people whose nerves have grown out of their scalps like hair, multicolored nerves like telephone wire twisting into abstract bouquets.

I don't know that I can tell their stories truly. The threads of their narratives are just out of my grasp. Their stories are the story of the darkness itself, and how could I ever hope to get my arms around that?

But I'm going to try, because this is what we do.

Through my life I've tried to capture more and more of the invisible world. I struggle to tell the truth as I understand it. I look for the moment that tells. Melanie and I write this biography of our imaginations. We create a testament of what we felt, what we saw and what we imagined that we saw, what we heard when the sound was turned off, how it was to be here this relatively short time on ground that could barely hold us down.

It may not be the best thing, it may not have been the best way, but you do the best you can. You do what it is you do. And this is what we do.

So much happens in a life. More than we can remember. More than we can hold. Sometimes we repeat ourselves in order to retrieve the moments we have lost.

The images we do recall fade like old film. We reimagine the colors and put them back into the reel, and when we view them again they're *close* to the original, but not quite the same.

One day Anthony and I walked together around the outside of the house. I let my arm dangle and spread my fingers until my hand practically covered his chest. He grabbed my arm and held on tight: little boy swinging on a vine. I could feel his heart in my hand as we raced through the jungle of the afternoon. Recalling, I could bend and smell his hair, that little boy smell of soap and perspiration, I could kiss his cheek and breathe in the coolness. I am that close.

Sometimes I think I should be through this, I should be over this, but I know that's not what I really want. I want him alive in my imagination.

Right after Anthony died, I wanted to believe in an afterlife where I would see him at least one more time, where I would see him. But no matter how hard I tried I couldn't quite imagine that and I felt as if I'd let him down.

My baby. You hold their small hearts, their lungs in your hands and it is unimaginable: both their lives and their deaths are unimaginable. How they came to be out of nothing and how this miracle has been put into your undeserving hands to nourish or to fail. Sometimes it brings the absolute best out of people and sometimes the absolute worst. I've seen people snap under the pressure, we've all seen them, dissolving in the presence of a miracle.

There is my boy running in the woods wearing a yellow windbreaker and rich brown corduroy pants. There, and no, over there. He is there, and there, until I can't see him any longer, no matter how hard I try I can't reach him.

Looking at the ground, I see people filling every mound and curvature of the earth. As far as the eye can see and far beyond, I see them turning in their sleep.

Looking out into the woods, I see a shape frozen inside every tree, weeping or praying or simply waiting for the next movement of the dance, angels and demons and sometimes it doesn't matter which. Miracles, waiting for just the right moment to raise their ancient bowed heads and meet my gaze.

I come so close sometimes. I come so close.

For so long I have lived on the edge of an invisible world. Sometimes I feel like the scattered debris left over after the personality has fallen out of the sky.

Some nights I rise from the bed and climb into the dark envelope that will take me, if I'm lucky, safely down the stairs.

Sometimes I wait at the bottom of those dark stairs, I sit at the bottom of the stairs, I wait beyond the bottom of the stairs and listen to the sounds my wife and children make as they sleep, the sounds our animals make as they step carefully through our dreams and out the other side to polished floor and cold window. Sometimes I wait so long I become unsure if I am asleep, or awake, or dead.

Down here in the dark, everything we tried to forget has become familiar again. Pale glimpses of children pad lazily around, thumbs wedged into their mouths, looking for their names. In the highly-charged dark, they wave like translucent grasses underwater.

My friend here is someone whose nerves have grown several inches outside her head. I'm curious as to how she feels, if she keeps in touch with another world, if she hears the same sounds I hear coming from my children's bedrooms, if she knows which way the wind is going to blow. If she really knows. Anything.

But down here in the dark, questions hardly matter. Down here in the dark, you can sit all night with someone and never speak.

Down here in the dark, you can wonder how you ever kept going on with it, how you got up every day to go wherever it was you were required to go. You can't even remember what you did all those hours so just how important was it to do those things you did?

The figure whose nerves now halo and massage her head floats up out of the chair beside me. Patches and threads of skin tear away where they've grown into the seat. They float around in the air as if they were nothing. She stretches out her legs and kicks in slow motion, moving across the room as if huge and unstoppable. Until I stop her by speaking her name.

This is the way it happens, even though I do not hear myself speak her name, even though I have no idea what I just said.

For down here in the dark, names are more important than ever, even though we do not know the names, or hear ourselves speaking.

Down here in the dark, a fish floats by with holes where its eyes should be. You can see all the way through into the darkness on the other side. Then the fish turns its body toward you and you know it is seeing you through those dark holes.

"Where are you?" Melanie whispers from the top of the stairs.

"We're all down here, in the dark," I reply. And she goes back to bed. There is nothing she can do about this. Everything that happens here is necessary. Everything we're telling you here is true.

I have to admit that sometimes I suffer from a certain inattentiveness. For brief moments I seem to forget where I am and who I am and what was the last thing my children said to me. I forget to take care of my body and I forget there is traffic, there is always traffic to contend with. Sometimes

I just don't know. Sometimes I'm just down here in the dark.

Melanie or the kids will ask me, "Where are you?" and I will say "sorry" or "right here" because I don't want to tell them I'm down here in the dark. I don't know how to explain that, as much as I love them, some things and some places must remain mine alone. And I don't want to remind them that there are similar dark places waiting for them.

Down beyond the bottom of the stairs is my rabbit's warren of an office, half buried in the ground and wrapped in the dry smell of books. Here is where I ride the dark down every night, when I can't sleep, when I wonder about what's waiting for me, when I long for the surprise of words felt through my fingers and displaying on the shimmering white screen.

Down here in the dark, I forget where I am and I forget when I am and sometimes I ride through all night typing and typing and forcing the words to lie down. If Melanie wakes up before I go to bed, she comes down worried I might have died in my office through the course of this long night.

I never know what to say to her. I'm sorry I made her worry. But I had words to lay down—they had become far too heavy to bear. That's why I came down here in the dark, into the home of the thing with the long nerves for hair and the boy who cannot remember his name.

This is why all the walls here are yellow, why sometimes these fish turn upside down and drown in the weight of their remorse. Sometimes there's not much to do, down here in the dark, but wait.

I want to tell Melanie, I want to tell the kids don't worry, there's nothing to worry about here, everything will be okay. But I can't say this because I of all people know better. Even out-of-shape, absent-minded fellows like myself—good fellows, good-natured as you would want—do die, do pitch forward onto their keyboards. They do reach and overbalance and fall and fall, not hitting the floor until they are cold. The shadow fishes all scatter and wait. The dark ones with nerves for hair sit and watch, all their bits floating as if submerged in that fluid we all live in.

This one, this dark lover of mine kisses me and

tickles my brain. She gazes at me as if to say *so what are you going to do what are you going to do?*

I can't promise anything. Down here in the dark, I don't know what else to say. Melanie, I don't know what else to say.

And Melanie, who knows me better than anyone, who knows me better sometimes than I know myself, tells me, "You don't have to say anything. So much is beyond words, though so much can in fact be said. Words are among the most beautiful of the masks of God, but they are not God, my love.

"If you don't know what else to say, write about not knowing what else to say. We can just float, wise as fish, in the wordless space of not knowing and not saying, with holes for letting the darkness flow through.

"Wise as fish. Wise as a yellow cat, a coiled snake. Spacious as wilderness twilight; wise and spacious as the house we open for anything to happen in, whatever will happen.

"We don't have to say anything, sweetheart. We don't have to understand. Things don't have to mean anything. The horizontal line doesn't ever have to intersect with the vertical. We can just float.

"Float in the certainty that things fall out of the sky. Float in the presence of the man on the ceiling. Float in the incomprehensible presence of our child's death, which means everything and doesn't have to *mean* anything other than itself."

There's always too much to say. There's always too much. Once you've allowed yourself to travel in the dark, you understand how much we do not say, because to do so might be in poor taste or impolite or foolish, or in order to deny what slithers and creeps right under our noses, or in order to give it space.

An elderly friend once told me the worst thing about growing old was the *rudeness* of it all. The body doesn't breathe or digest properly, water is retained and water is expelled, you stink like a leaky furnace and you drip urine and your breath smells bad. You can't drink enough water to keep things lubricated and still you're going to the bathroom all the time, just begging for yet another incident to feel shame over. You swell with the riches of edema, and gravity has so changed its attitude it threatens with every step to wrestle you into immobility.

These are among the subjects polite people don't discuss. Down here in the dark, let me tell you it stinks. Down here in the dark, it stinks of cruel impulse and foul inattention and everything you eat bears that faint aroma of despair. I'd ask my friend how he felt today. For a very long time he'd reply "tolerable" and "tolerable" until there came that day he replied "intolerable," and I can't remember too much of his final days but that "intolerable" has always stuck. The dark down here is full of knowledge of the intolerable.

I should be better than this I should be used to this but some things, some losses, are intolerable.

A woman who had read my stories once asked me, "But doesn't it make you *sad*, so terribly, terribly *sad?*" I remember mouthing platitudes about how the dark makes us appreciate the light more, how it increases the magnitude of the joy when there is joy, and this was all true, as far as I am able to discern the truth.

What I tried not to say to her was, "Of course it's

sad. Some things *are* terribly, terribly sad." And perhaps the strangest thing is that I've still been able to find the beauty in it, no matter how awful, how intolerable it becomes. Down here in the dark.

Down here in the dark, I close my eyes and the boy without a name pads across the carpet and whispers into my ear. I don't know if this is my son or someone else's son. When Anthony died I felt willing to do anything if I could just spend a few more minutes with him. For weeks my fictional output consisted of possible bargains I might make with God or the Fates or the Biological Prime Movers or whoever or whatever controlled such life and death matters for us unfortunate mortals. Maybe I could trade my sanity for one hour more of my son's time. Maybe there was something I could destroy as a kind of sacrifice. Maybe I could burn down this house, this place I have loved so long, take it down into ashes, take it down to ground, take it down into the dark with me. Or maybe if I gave up speech, or no, what if I gave up writing? If I swore I'd never compose another word for whatever remained of my life, then would they give me back my son?

But I didn't believe in gods or fates or movers prime or otherwise. I had a head full of elaborate, even beautiful prayers and no one to submit them to.

So over the years there was nowhere for my son to go but into my stories, and into the smaller, hidden rooms of my imagination. Not always obvious or particularly identifiable, but a character presence just the same.

Down here this little boy tells me to leave him alone to please just let him be.

But down here in the dark, I am king. No one can tell me what to do. Down here in the dark, I sit on my throne of failing flesh and I wear a crown and jewels of swarming, dancing flies. Sometimes their buzzing is so loud I can hardly hear the weeping that fills these rooms late at night after everyone else has gone to bed.

But I do hear. And I realize this is as far as I can go, this is as far as anyone should ever ask me to go. So I take this child and I tuck him into the wall, the flaps of plaster gone rubbery as they wind him in like a sheet.

After five kids I'm tired and I'm done, at least

that's the way I'd been thinking. I can't say we're not tempted, both of us—for me a few years ago it was the little dark girl with the deformed face who would require multiple surgeries to effect a transformation that still wouldn't make her look like everybody else. For Melanie it was a more recent encounter with an honest-to-God feral child. That temptation comes in large part because these are kids we know we could take care of, but I have to admit it's also because they have an air of the mythic about them, of having just stepped out of some dark fairytale, and dark fairytales are something Melanie and I can appreciate.

But I'm tired, I'm heading into my late fifties and I know that time has passed for me. So what am I doing with this little boy? What am I thinking about here? And how am I going to explain him to our other children?

Not because it's smart. Not because I'm being a good father. Not even because I have the faintest clue what I'm doing. But because it's my responsibility. Because it's what I'm supposed to do. Because it's what I do.

But when I try to look into this child's face one last time I see that he is gone. I look around at these walls: flesh or stone or something in between, and I can hear his child's laughter just on the other side. Only stone separates us. Only stone and dirt and the years of used-up memories separate us. Only his skin separates us. And I close my eyes and hold my breath and push on through.

Once inside this other geometry, this alternate architecture of our house, I'm surprised I'm not better prepared for it. After all, haven't I imagined and re-imagined this place between places hundreds of times? Haven't I walked here in my dreams? And who better to see it than someone who has worked on this old structure for more than two decades, peeked under the floorboards, excavated its lath and plaster walls, studied its wiring and plumbing, peeled back its skins of paint and wallpaper to find the face it wore for its first owners? But I didn't see this coming.

My boy without a name is still in sight, still clinging to what passes for a ceiling here (roots and sheets of moss, hair of a thousand heads, an infectious whispering from the dark jewelry of insect life that toils and boils and clings there, and discarded toys once too precious to name, now irretrievable from the greedy grip of time) and I hold my breath waiting for him to fall, waiting in fact for it all to come down, for there is absolutely nothing holding all this up, there is nothing holding him, or any of the rest of us for that matter, as high as our dreams or nightmares seek to take us.

Yet he manages to defy gravity as we all do, so I take a first cautious step in my attempt to follow him, my shoe sinking into the rotting tissue of the eight hundred thirty-two sheets that have sheathed the beds of this house over a hundred years, grabbing onto railings wired together from antique broom handles, hobby horses, and greasy candlesticks, my fingers scraping through a thick cushion of dust that itself murmurs and sings, and time here is a cold draft that steals my breath, and I stumble forward desperate to catch it again.

I call up to my lovely boy, "Wait! Please!" and he turns and grins playfully, as if this at last is the best game he'd always been denied. I can't help but smile back at him because nothing's better than when a lonely child manages to play.

And this is the way it is for us as we pass up one level and down three more, sideways for a time and then it's me crawling across the ceiling, my head hanging down like a broken knob, and he's the one chasing below and trying name after Rumpelstiltskin name none of which I recognize because no one ever cared enough to give me one that fit well enough not to fall off. So I crawl ahead naked of name but I know it could be worse.

Then it's me chasing again, not sure if it's a real chase or just hide-and-seek, speed encumbered by the desire never to let the playtime end. I push my way past lamps that don't work and the myriad traps that do, tiny rooms encapsulating that one great moment—whatever it was, whenever it happened—that if you're not careful will harden into a defining moment and you'll let yourself stay there the rest of your life.

The strangest thing, I must admit, is that it's not so strange at all. Who among us can manage a life in the present for more than fifteen minutes at a time? So often living in the present is like sticking your head under water: the scenery is new and the light is different but sooner or later you have to jerk your head back into the atmosphere you know and think you understand.

Down here in the dark is the life every house knows from birth until final destruction. Down here in the dark is every chair, every plate, every spoon this home has housed, every coat hung up in haste, every shirt cast off in passion, every spoiled handkerchief and every injured shoe. Down here are the hats without reason, the mirrors unseeing, the sad doll in the windowsill, the letters unmailed and more unanswered. Here are the prizes we'd hoped for and the tears whose tracks gather dust.

I'm tired past sleep but so worried this child will hurt himself, even though I know they all do, and will, however much you shout into their faces and wring the juice from your own hands. I push myself forward through the ever-rising tide of my life's debris and reach for him, reach for him begging him to come down. But he's having so much fun, maybe for the first time ever—he thinks every obstacle is a game now and every word I push his way just another aspect of the joke.

The walls here are board and paste and horse-hair, then ages of plastered yellow newspaper to cover the chinks, then I'm rushing past graffiti, exclamations of bored despair and love notes to the world, then stretch after stretch of wallpaper, some I recognize as coverings I had stripped away, and in one long hall from the twenties, yellow fish in a vast green sea, the fish shapes drift in and out of the wall surface keeping pace with me, now and again vanishing completely, only to pop their heads right out of the wall on my next step, their mouths open with the astonishment of my presence.

The walls grow color and melt. The walls spin tumble dry low. In this more complicated home I am the intruder, my claims of ownership a child's whine after dinner when dessert is denied.

Out of the moments ago behind me two women with beautiful heads of cascading nerve come float-ing. One stretches a pale, stick-like limb across my shoulders as if to comfort me. The other lays finger to lips. *This is the time,* she offers softly, as the other peels my suddenly sleeping boy off the ceiling and settles him at my feet. *This is the time.*

Of course it is. It gathers itself around us, it sneaks past us like a criminal on the run. It's always one step ahead but six steps behind.

Sometimes we get so close. Sometimes we almost know. But things don't stop, things don't stop, not even when breath weakens and falls behind.

Down here in the dark, things don't stop.

11
EVERYTHING WE'RE TELLING YOU HERE IS TRUE

This is the closest I can get.

Melanie and I tell our stories expecting some meaning in the end. We tell ourselves this is all going somewhere. Sometimes we get so close, reach so far, we can smell it from over the mountain, we can see flashes of it in the distant sunlight, we can almost make out the faces in the photographs, and where the lines split apart, and what they reveal.

Often we do not choose our stories, but our stories choose us.

* ، ★ ، ★

Once upon a time, I can't quite find Steve. He's here and he's somewhere else.

This story is as true as I know it to be. It's my story, not his.

I'm afraid of secrets. But also, secrets fascinate and reassure me. Steve is full of secrets, though he's the most open and accessible man I've ever known. He welcomes me closer and closer, and knowing that there will always be a space between his story line and mine is part of the richness of the life we keep discovering together. Even when it scares me to death.

I imagine a story similar to what I guess he might be thinking about, and then I see if he's there. If I find him, if I manage to come as close to finding him as anyone ever finds anyone, I might tell him to come home for dinner. Or I might see if I can go with him, into a story that includes us both. Or, if I'm strong enough, I might let him go.

Once upon a time, I might let him go.

When I look back at the words I have written to Melanie and myself, the stories that have tumbled out of that collision of the real and the dream and the dream that is real, I realize I didn't mean to tell so much and I didn't mean to tell so little. But this is my testament. This is our imaginations' biography, and our job is to feed it what it needs, and sometimes what it needs is for us to let go, to surrender our need for you to think of us as wise or happy or sane. Sometimes what it needs is our very lives.

Once upon a time. Once upon a time we get so close, we get so close. That's the mystery of it, the romance and the fantasy, the horror.

Ask the man on the ceiling. But don't count on him telling you what you wanted to hear. Don't count on him answering you at all.

Sometimes not getting there is half the fun. I believe Melanie has known this for some time. I used to think you had to *arrive*, otherwise you weren't going anywhere. More and more we understand how the music comes from the pulse of blood through the body, the movement of muscle across bone, the coming and going of events, the people who pass in and out of immediate personal space. The line of it goes up and up and up, closer and closer to whatever other line there is, that first heart-rending tone of "Rhapsody in Blue," the single acoustic guitar and the huge concert organ playing note for note and coming close to each other but never quite blending, the cello like the movement of the storyteller under the earth.

The demons and the angels cooped up in the house have to be taken out for a walk now and then, so they can run around on the grass, smell the other creatures who've been there, relieve themselves. It's not always much fun, but it is something I can do, which makes it my responsibility to do it.

Later, when Melanie finally gets into the car, she apologizes for keeping me waiting. There was something she had to take care of in the attic or in the basement, some story she's been waiting for that finally came to her and she had to write it down, some dream that wouldn't let her wake up, some last-minute good-byes she had to say.

Our trips are shorter these days. I can't drive as long or as far as I used to, and driving at night is harder because the lights tend to bother me and there are lines crisscrossing everywhere. That's okay; I never really enjoyed driving anyway. Melanie has ideas for our future travels, such as the Grand Canyon. I say to her, "Are you crazy? All those cliffs and drop-offs?" And you can bet I'm not getting on a burro.

I like nothing better than staying at home. But

I know that getting out now and again is good for me. We settle back in our seats, fasten our seatbelts, smile at each other. I start the car.

We pass the line of children slowly, knowing how children can be careless. They wrestle and shove each other. They don't pay attention. They run into things. They put ropes around their necks that become nooses. They fall.

I check out the back seat. It's amazing the amount of equipment people take along. Special pillows. Extra blankets. Extra socks. Cameras and flash attachments and film, as if a moment could be captured. And kids. It seems there have always been, and always will be, the kids. I'm not sure who we have with us this day. When they sleep, as they so often do on these road trips, they look like they were when they were little. They resemble themselves, and they resemble their own children, down to the exact angle at which a mouth hangs open, the exact same placement of a hand. And despite the fact that they have come to us in such different ways, from such different worlds, I always find it remarkable how much they resemble each other. And us.

There's still a little room left in the car. There's always a little room left.

Ahead of us on the side of the road is a small boy with light brown hair and glasses. For a time after Anthony died I noticed little boys who looked like him everywhere, and I tried to take that as evidence that there'd been a mistake at the hospital, some sort of trick, a variant on the apocryphal story of babies being switched at birth—it was somebody else's son who'd died, not ours, and I was sorry for those parents, but Anthony, Anthony, Anthony was alive. Story after story I made up, but none of them was in any sense true.

I slow down the car, then stop. I can no longer look at the boy, but Melanie gasps and I see the expression on her face. The back door opens, I hear him slide onto the seat, the door slams.

Not knowing what else to do, I put the car into drive again, moving away from this line of children with their pale faces and pitiful belongings. In the rearview mirror I see there are more than ever, and I see that the car behind us is going to stop.

Anthony is singing to himself, a favorite sound,

that music children make for themselves when they're pleased about something. Scared, I look at him in the rearview mirror as long as I can stand it. His little glasses are crooked. He always had a hard time keeping them on straight. Weeping silently, I'm afraid I won't be able to drive.

"It's okay," Melanie says softly beside me, patting my leg.

"Do we tell him? Do we need to tell him?" I wipe my eyes with the back of my hand.

"I don't know," she says. She's crying, too. "I don't know." And that's all we say about it as we head on down the road. All I can be sure of is that he has no other life than this, no other life beyond what Melanie and I can imagine.

After a while I find I can look into the mirror again: Anthony asleep by the window, his fine blondish hair blowing across his glasses. Beside him Gabriella has stretched out her long legs, her mouth pursed in sleep as if dreaming solutions to some complicated math. Joe has his arms crossed, his eyes tightly shut, holding it all in. Chris sleeps the sleep of the innocent, his face soft and at last untroubled. Veronica lies curled at one end of the seat, her legs drawn up in a fetal position, and again I am amazed at how much she contains, yet how small the space she can occupy.

I reach up and adjust the mirror, moving it about dangerously, one eye on the road ahead as I look for them, for I know they must be there. And yes, piled up like puppies, Sophia, Mya, Katy, and Christiana, our granddaughters.

* * ★ * ★

Later we will speak. We will tell them stories. We will tell them this story. Everything we tell them will be true.

About the Authors

Steve Rasnic Tem has been called "a school of writing unto himself" (Joe R. Lansdale). His surreal stories have earned him comparisons to Franz Kafka, Dino Buzzati, Ray Bradbury, and Raymond Carver. As a solo writer and editor he has won the Bram Stoker, British Fantasy, and International Horror Guild awards, and been nominated for the Philip K. Dick and World Fantasy awards.

Award-winning author, poet, and playwright Melanie Tem is the author of fourteen published novels. Her works have won, among many accolades, the Bram Stoker Award and the British Fantasy Award. Dan Simmons called her "the literary successor to Shirley Jackson," and readers and reviewers consistently rave about her deeply involved stories of the terrors that haunt families.

Together, Melanie and Steve won the Bram Stoker Award for their multi-media collection *Imagination Box*, and won a Stoker, International Horror Guild, and World Fantasy award for their novella "The Man on the Ceiling" (the only work ever to win all three). They live in Denver, Colorado with the family they have made for themselves.

The Man on the Ceiling has been set in Bell MT, a 1931 Monotype facsimile of the typeface cut by Richard Austin in 1788 for John Bell's newspaper *The Oracle*.